Your Boyfriend is Hot 2
ISBN 978-1-911478-30-0
Copyright©2019 Barry Lowe
Cover art and design by Dawné Dominique

Published by
Lydian Press 2019
Find us on the World Wide Web at
www.lydianpress.com

YOUR BOYFRIEND IS HOT 2

Gay Cuckold Erotica

Barry Lowe

Lydian Press

CONTENTS

1   A SIX-PACK FOR SAMSON

29   SOLD BY MY STEPDAD

59   VALENTINE'S WAY

109   WHAT TIME DOES YOUR BOYFRIEND GET HOME?

Mind if we borrow your boyfriend?

A SIX-PACK FOR SAMSON

I was horny as fuck and you can't get much hornier than that. My boyfriend, Brad, has been away for the past ten days on an important mission with the firm he works for. Not just him but the department head and four of the top alphas in the premier investment corporation, Safe-as-Houses Investment Inc. Brad is new to the company which flaunts its conservative credentials by boasting it never (knowingly) employed one of 'them radical femmenazis or uppity homo-sexualists.' I add the word 'knowingly' because Brad is as gay as rainbow glitter and twice as proud – except when it comes to keeping the best paid job of his career.

He doesn't like it any more than I do but sometimes you have to play by the company's rules in order to get ahead. I'm giggling. I just wrote 'head.' Which immediately makes me think of head jobs and how much I love sucking Brad's brains out through his dick. It's been waaay too long. I need his cock – like right now.

But I have to wait. He texted me he's on his way home. His is a tense, stressful job which is why I like to be lubed up and ready to help him relax. That's one of the only two things that have that effect on him. My cute, gym-toned body and insatiable bubble butt is one. And the company's well-equipped gym where he can work off his irritation and frustrations is the second. Fuck, now just thinking about well-equipped (FYI: Brad is extraordinarily well-equipped) has my ass pulsing in expectation. So, also FYI, Brad has the body of an Adonis and the looks to complement it. The perfect fit to my prettier rather than masculine looks, augmented by my long hair that has me often mistaken for a woman. There were ample compensations to my appearance before I met Brad because quite a few bi-curious gents in my aerobics classes decided I was as good a shot as any to sate their curiosity. Happy days.

Not that I'm not happy now. But ten days missing your man can lead to a lot of nostalgia for the good old days of quick anonymous shags and ass-warping gangbangs. Now all that frustration is about to end. Brad is on his way home and we have our ingenious method by which I welcome him back. We created it on one of those occasions when our sex life had deteriorated into that jaded same-old, same-old. We took our relationship by the bootstraps and shook it about, considering every permutation from kink to kennel to kinesiology. My eyes glazed over and I was breathless when we discussed opening up our relationship or adding a third – neither of us had ever cheated – but even though Brad looked at my reaction strangely, he'd passed on that variation. I guess that was the right thing to do.

Had we gone that route there was plenty to choose from. Guys at the gym were forever hitting on me and ditto for Brad in his line of work even though he was playing it straight. But my ass remained tightly zipped except when Brad was around. So here I am, spread-eagled on our leather lounge, my ankles held in stirrups that we'd screwed into the back so I can recline, ass aimed at the front door. That way the first thing Brad sees on coming home is my puckered hole ready for his tongue or his cock. It makes me feel incredibly sexy but also totally depraved. I love it.

I wriggled into position, my legs spread wide, as soon as Brad texted me he was on his way, hours later than I'd expected. Because the mission had been so successful they'd stopped off for a little celebratory refreshment. I hoped not too celebratory as to make Brad incapable of pleasuring the hot ass awaiting him at home. A few drinks and he loses all inhibitions and can screw for hours. Just one extra drink and it's limp noodle cock city.

The stirrups were mighty comfortable and I must have dozed off because the next thing I know there's the sound of a key in the front door. I wriggled into my favorite position, attempting to get the slight cramp out of my left leg – I didn't want to be grimacing when Brad caught sight of me. I flexed my ass muscles to make sure they were good and tight, and waited, a come hither smile plastered on my face. I know how to please my man. Hell, if I'm honest, I know how to please any man.

"Welcome…" The greeting died on my lips. It wasn't Brad who came through the door. It was one his co-workers. The boss's nephew, Colt, the biggest asshole of Safe-as-Houses Investment Inc. Colt was his nickname because he had turned 45 that year and thought he was still hot as a pistol although every time he blew a load he shot blanks. He'd had the snip because he was a bit too free with the ladies. He was also carried by the men in his department because he was too lazy to work for his powerful position – he believed he didn't need to. Nepotism was his Get-Out-of-Jail Free card. That counted for a lot.

I knew what Brad's co-workers looked like because I'd stumbled on them all making quite a rowdy nuisance of themselves in a bar where I'd arranged to meet him after work in the first few weeks of his employment. The look on his face said it all – Do Not Approach. I didn't. I sat at the bar and watched the group. The guys were all attractive although one or two of them were carrying more weight than necessary – a result of too many fast food lunches? Colt, in particular was ripped. His business suit and button down shirt scarcely contained a body that was related to the proverbial brick shithouse. But he was arrogant with it, a real turn-off for me.

As soon as the group departed, Brad made up for ignoring me initially with the most romantic dinner ever! Followed by the best dessert in the world – his load down my throat. In the best place ever – in the restaurant. I pretended to drop my napkin and crawled under the table – I was well hidden by the linen cloth – and sucked him until his orgasm was so intense he almost blew a hole in the back of my throat.

Colt stopped dead just inside the door. "What the fuck."

There was a murmur of other voices as Brad's workmates pushed into the room.

"Wish my wife would greet me like that after a hard day at the office," Marty grumbled. He was married to one of the most gorgeous women in the city — yep, Safe-as-Houses Investments Inc liked its employees married — but she was less than affectionately known as Ms. Frozen around the office.

I struggled to get free and cover my very obvious erection (when the hell had that happened?) and especially my hot, lubed inviting asshole but all I managed was to get myself impossibly

4

tangled in the stirrups and the more I thrashed about the worse I made the situation.

"Sorry, mate. Wrong house," Ken, the quiet one, said, attempting to usher the others back out the door.

Colt shoved him out of the way. "Fuck that. This is Brad's house. Must be. The key fit. So what the hell is that fag doing laid out on the couch like a Christmas turkey with his ass dripping like it's spunk gravy?"

Spunk gravy? Really? Who says that?

I'd taken a blood oath on pain of death that I would never do anything to embarrass Brad in front of his boss and co-workers – not that we thought I would ever meet them, especially not like this. His future employment depended on it and I was known sometimes for my more, let's just say, outrageous and flamboyant behavior. And what could be more outrageous and flamboyant than being trussed up on the lounge, legs akimbo, hard cock oozing pre-cum and my asshole twitching with desire? Kill me now.

Of course, being homophobic assholes that outcome was quite possible at the hands of these social Neanderthals.

No-one made an effort to untangle me, put me out of my misery, or allow me to cover my…I was about to call it shame but a better description would have been excitement. Not often I find myself helplessly displayed in front of a group of guys who were glaring at me like a particularly nasty shit floating in the bowl.

Going for nonchalance, I croaked, "Um, where's Brad?"

Colt pushed the group inside before closing the door. "He went to get beer so we can keep on celebrating the completion of our greatest contract ever. Gave us the keys and told us to make ourselves at home." He looked puzzled. "So if this is Brad's house what the hell are you doing here?"

Think fast. "Um…I'm one of his mates."

Some of the men snickered.

Colt just got more belligerent. "Yeah? You always greet your mates like that? Nah, don't bother answering that. You're one of those slutty fags who think any straight man is easy pickings just by flashing your tight asshole, right?"

"Had experience, have you?" I never know when to keep my mouth shut.

He was across the room, slapped my ass so hard it must have left a red imprint, then grabbed me around the throat and squeezed. His arm brushed my cock and I dribbled more pre-cum onto his shirt sleeve. "What the fuck?" He wiped the sleeve across my face. "Filthy fuckin' pervert." He went to strike me across the face but Ken swiftly intercepted and held him back.

The other men looked about ready to bolt. Ken tried herding them out, "Come on, guys. Let's go. Brad'll sort it out."

"We're not going anywhere. There's something fucked going on here."

Oh, oh. I knew Colt detested Brad because he was new to the company but already incredibly successful in attracting valuable extra business, to the detriment of Colt's reputation. No love lost there. I knew the others were middle-range brokers who probably seethed quietly that the new boy made them look ordinary. Not that any of them were now that I could see them close up in their disheveled business attire. They'd obviously been celebrating hard and were a little the worse for wear. That made them unpredictable. Dangerous.

The guys were buzzing. I tried covering my ass and my genitals in between attempting to wrestle the stirrups. To no avail. "How about you give me a hand and I'll get you all something to nibble on and some coffee."

"I have something here you can nibble on," Colt sneered drawing attention to the outline of what he was packing by stroking it. "You'd like that, wouldn't you fag? A real man's cock to suck?" I'm only human, my mouth watered and my ass twitched.

"How about I give him a hand?" Dil, the nastiest looking of the bunch, said crossing the room. *Thank you, Dil.* I relaxed. Prematurely as it transpired because Dil's idea of a hand was a sharp open-handed swat against my exposed ass cheeks. Not satisfied with one he gave me an even half dozen until my cheeks reddened and I felt so exposed and vulnerable I shuddered. These guys couldn't mean any real harm because Brad would be home shortly and I would...

"Fuckin' fags." He spat in my face.

Trust me, I couldn't help taunting him by stretching out my tongue to lick as much of it away as I could reach. Strange, I noticed a slight lengthening in the outline of his cock highlighted by his tighter than normal trousers that also drew attention to his tight muscular ass.

The others, emboldened by Colt and Dil's behavior pressed forward.

Colt was still having problems attempting to put the pieces together in his brain – probably not helped by having the image of my inviting asshole seared into his eyeballs. Bingo. The lights came on. His smirk was evil. "Where's Brad's wife, you pervert?"

"Fuck you?" I yelled, then fell right into the trap. "What wife?"

His smile said everything. "Brad told us he was married. Did he lie on his application to get the job. Hm, that's a sackable offence."

There was no way out of the situation. "No, he didn't lie."

"Then where's his missus?" Marty asked. They didn't seem to have puzzled it out quite yet although I was sure Colt had.

"I'm his missus," I sighed.

"What the fuck?" Logan squawked.

"How can that be?" Marty asked. "You do drag or something?"

How do you deal with Neanderthal city? "No, I don't do drag."

Marty turned to the others. "He'd make a pretty girl." When he saw their reaction he backtracked. "Not that I'd fuck him, even in a dress."

Logan persisted. "So how can you be his wife?"

"You forget we just had a very expensive and unnecessary postal vote about marriage equality?" I paused to stop my mouth from going where it shouldn't. Too late. "Oops, silly me, I forgot you probably don't know how to make a tick in a box so you probably didn't vote at all."

He went red in the face. "You know what we do to fags like you?"

Sarcasm is not your friend in a situation like this. "Let me guess, you fuck 'em up real bad. Put 'em in hospital. Makes you feel hyper masculine."

If looks could kill.

Colt came to my rescue. "Don't scare him."

That did scare the bejeezus out of me. Colt obviously had a much more painful option in mind. Something that would screw both me and Brad.

"Look, leave Brad out of this and you can do what you want to me." I had visions of ending up in hospital, my bones broken, my pretty face battered. It was a small price to pay.

Colt patted me on the head. "We can do what we want with you anyway, mate. You can't get away." Turning to the others, "None of you guys like Brad, right?" There were mumbles of agreement only Logan loudly vocal in his response. "He's been an asshole since the day he started. Making us look bad. Always going on about his perfect home life. Well, you can see how perfect his home life is spread out in front of us. Perverted fagdom, that's his home life. You know what the company thinks of fags. Hell, it reflects what we think of fags. Right?"

More mumbles of agreement. "Right?" Colt yelled in an attempt to rally the troops.

They shouted on demand. Fuckin' sheep. I could see why Brad was the best in his department after just a few months.

Colt purred. "Normally we'd fuck over a fag like this one." He yanked my long hair for emphasis. "If he complained to the police we'd just use that old standby: 'Gee, officer, the fag propositioned me, made a grab for the family jewels. I saw red and panicked. Beat the shit out of the little fucker.' Gay panic defense. The company's expensive legal team would convince everyone we were heroes for beating up the little fag." The group looked as if they'd be up for that. "But," he continued, pausing for effect. "In order to do that we gotta stick together. Get our stories straight."

They were talking about me as if I wasn't even there although Colt was running his hand across my ass cheeks. I couldn't help it, I shuddered. My cock drooled. Okay, so I'm a shallow slut. How could I be turned on when this was my life, or at least serious injury, they were talking about.

"But," Colt said ominously, "what if rather than fuck this fag over we just fuck him?"

I was just as surprised as the others, some of whom looked a little green at the idea.

"No, hear me out guys. I know you aren't fags but a tight asshole is second only to a tight cunt." There spoke a man from experience. "Okay, so it's not a chick's ass but flip the fag over and with his long hair you'd swear it was a chick's hole."

Yeah, right, as long as you can ignore the cock and balls dangling between my legs. I may be somewhat femme and twinky but there's a fair bit of man meat down there. Not that I was about to interrupt Colt's fantasy.

"That way we get to ruin this fag's asshole. Show him how real men, straight men, fuck. Hard and deep. Wreck him big time by the time we finish. Fill him full of manjuice, fuck his throat until he chokes. Cover his face with our spunk." Colt was definitely getting off on his little fantasy. His voice became huskier, the effect hypnotic, as he described what the group could do to me in the way of sexual depravity, some of the men falling under the spell, surreptitiously adjusting their package.

"The pretty little fag will enjoy it. Even if he doesn't, who the fuck cares? We'll relieve a lot of our fuckin' tension in his ass, and we'll destroy not only this fag cunt but Brad as well and his perfect relationship. We'll send pictures of the fag out on social media after we've fucked him. When Brad comes home and sees his so-called wife covered in our spunk we'll tell him his boyfriend begged for it. Relationship over. Plus we'll let management know that Brad's so-called marriage is a farce. Brad's career? Also over."

Logan was first. "I'm in."

Some of the others took a little more convincing.

"You don't have to fuck him," Colt said. "But look what you'll be missing out on." He slid two fingers into my asshole. The penetration took me by surprise and I arched my back which forced my ass down on his fingers so he penetrated even deeper.

"So fuckin' tight," Colt cooed. "It'll be a real pleasure to split him open. But choices, choices, look at his mouth. Soft cocksucking lips. I bet his throat is like velvet." For emphasis, he withdrew his fingers from my ass and ran them lightly across my lips before shoving them roughly in my mouth. They tasted of KY but I sucked them like my life depended on it. Colt was surprised by my enthusiasm but recovered quickly. "Hey, Marty, I know your missus don't give blowjobs but if it's one thing faggots are good at it it's giving head. Bet he can deep throat, swallow your cock down to your balls. If I'm any judge of character, he swallows." Marty shuddered at the thought. I ran my tongue along Colt's fingers as seductively as possible, showing off: I'd do anything to avoid a trip to the hospital. I might be able to save myself from physical harm but there was little hope for Brad's career or our relationship. Unless I could convince him I was coerced into what was to happen.

Colt was winding up his pitch. "And if his ass and his mouth don't tempt you, then just blow your load over his pretty face. Okay? This is all in or none in. We bash him there's gonna be repercussions though we'll win in the end. If we fuck him it's a win-win-win for us. We get our rocks off, we fuck his marriage, and Brad gets his career fucked. Everyone in?"

Dil was the remaining sceptic. "What if Brad walks in while we're doing his boyfriend?"

"Brad told us to make ourselves at home, and we wouldn't want to be ungrateful guests now would we?"

"I don't think this is what he had in mind," Dil mumbled.

Colt leaned forward and thrust two fingers back into my ass. It burned my entrance and I grunted. "The guy's panting for it. Look how his ass clenches round my fingers." Lucky I was well lubed or it would have hurt a lot more than it did. Like a trained performer I clenched my sphincter as he dragged his fingers out.

I was troubled by the glazed look in Logan's eyes. "I bet he could take a whole fist if he really tried." I looked at his large hairy hands. It would be like having a small domestic pet shoved inside me.

It was time to make my plea for mercy. "Come on, guys, you've had your fun embarrassing me. Now let me up and I'll get you coffee. Brad'll be home soon and…" I left the idea hanging because I had no idea how he'd react to his work mates slobbering over me naked. Let alone Colt's fingers playing concertos on my ass and an increasing number of bulges in men's tight trousers.

Colt snickered. "Brad will be gone for ages. Nothing's open around here so he'll have to go most of the way into town before he finds beer. By the time he gets back…" He didn't finish the sentence. He didn't have to. Had I been able to break free I could have escaped but with my feet tangled I had no hope. I was at their mercy. And, god help me, didn't that turn me on.

I'd put up a struggle for appearance's sake but in the end they could do what they wanted with me…and didn't it make me feel guilty that I wanted it too. Pity they were slow as buggery getting about it. Only Colt seemed really enthusiastic, the others hovering on the periphery waiting to see how things progressed.

If I couldn't escape then I'd do what it took to make the best of the situation. Maybe I could salvage our relationship if not Brad's job, but I'd have to step up my game if I wanted results before Brad got home. I knew exactly how far he'd have to drive to find a liquor store that was open this time of the night and approximately the time for the journey there and back.

WTF was Brad thinking? He knows how horny I get and that I'd be itching to get his cock inside me the moment he walked through the door. Amazing how forgetful a skinful of beer can make a boyfriend. Well, fuck him for being so careless. Nah, fuck me.

Time to get this show on the road. "He'll kill you bastards when he finds out. If you lay a finger on me—"

"How about a finger in you? Better yet, three fingers in you?" Colt laughed at his own joke.

"You better not think about shoving your cock in my ass. Brad'll massacre the lot of you."

Colt continued to massage my prostate making my cock slit ooze. "Gay guys like you are all sluts at heart. Can't get enough cock in your tight little holes. Fuckin' begging for it."

Dil looked queasy. "Boss, I think we should go. This has gone far enough. We got enough info on Brad to get his ass kicked from here to next year. You know Human Resources will have our jobs for sexual harassment if he complains."

Colt laughed loudly. "He won't complain. He'll be begging us to fuck him every which way by the time we finish. Look at him. Cock hard as nails, drooling at the thought of getting his prostate reamed by all your hard cocks."

I gave it my best theatrical sneer. "In your dreams, asshole."

"I'm a great believer in dreams coming true, slut" Colt spat back. "See if you can rustle up some booze, Marty. You guys pull up a few chairs and watch what happens when you make a slut gasp for it."

Dil, Logan and Ken perched themselves on the floor and in the armchairs nearby, drawing them closer to the action.

"Here, Ken, you take over while I get more comfortable."

Ken looked uncomfortable. "I dunno boss. It doesn't seem right."

Colt was having none of it. "Does it seem right that you'll be looking for a new career if you don't do what you're asked? I draw your attention to your contract that spelled out your obligations. 'And any tasks deemed necessary for the execution of your duties.' I think that's pretty straightforward."

Still Ken hesitated. "Look." Colt turned to the men. "If we all stick together nothing will come of this. We'll take a video of the slut begging to be fucked. We'll use it if Brad finds out 'cause this cock whore will never complain. He'll try to save his relationship if he can't save his boyfriend's job."

He must have read my mind. "You bastards," I growled in my butchest tones. "I'll get you for this. I'll have your asses on a plate."

Colt grabbed my throat again. "I don't think so, sweetheart. You're our little fuck toy for the next hour or so and you'll do what we say."

His threats just made my cock harder. "Or what, big man?"

Colt chuckled. "You'll get to see just how big a man I am."

I snorted my contempt but any response from Colt was cut short by Marty coming back into the living room with a couple of bottles, namely Brad's prize bourbon and Russian vodka. "There's no beer and no mixers but this should keep the party going." He put the liquor on the coffee table and went to retrieve glasses.

"This is more like it," Logan said, getting into the mood.

Marty returned with tumblers and packets of crisps and crackers and salsa dip that he'd scrounged from the pantry. It really was taking on a real party atmosphere. All we needed was a few crepe hats and streamers. Logan broke open the bourbon and took a huge swig as if he needed Dutch courage. Then he poured himself a large tumbler full of liquor. "Here, give me that," Colt demanded. Logan handed it over reluctantly, I thought.

The guys were helping themselves to liquor and snacks they seemed more interested in than in me. "Wanna give me a drink? Lying here with my ass on view is tiring work." That got their attention.

"Oh, don't worry," Colt replied. "We haven't forgotten you." He held the bottle to my lips and upended too much vodka down my gullet. It burned its way down my throat, my explosive choking cough almost bringing it all up again. Once I could control my gasping it certainly helped mellow me out.

Okay, deep breath. "So, who's the brave man that's gonna wreck my ass first?"

Nobody volunteered. I turned to Colt. "Guess that leaves you big man."

Shucking off his coat and pulling down the fly on his trousers, fumbling inside his briefs to extract a rather large cock that was already hard and throbbing, he said smugly, "It'll be my pleasure," he laughed. "And yours."

I guessed none of the guys wanted to strip naked in front of their co-workers although they must have in their workplace gym. This, of course, was a very different situation. Logan had his cock out, leisurely stroking it as he helped himself to chips and dip. I didn't think kissing was on the cards but I didn't want that salsa mouth round my dick. Not gonna happen.

"No fuckin' way are you getting that monster in my ass," I whined as Colt ran it up my crack. I was exaggerating. I'd taken bigger but a little flattery plus a dare would help move things along.

Colt just laughed and pushed the head of his cock against my slick hole. "No way," I screamed. "You fucker! Get that away from me. I'll scream." He pushed, sliding all the way inside me in one move. Yep, it did hurt a little because I'd flexed my sphincter in a show of keeping him out, giving him obstruction enough he'd think I was non-consenting. As he pushed forward I relaxed so he wouldn't damage me inside. A loud theatrical scream of "Fuck! Take it out. It's too big. You're ripping me open," played to his ego and also meant I could testify (not that it was ever likely to come to that) that he'd forced himself on me. Truth is, his cock felt good. More than good, damn him. I thrashed about as if attempting to escape which only managed to embed his cock farther inside my guts. I pushed my fists against his chest as if to ward him off but really just to grab his shirt and tear it open. He was a magnificent specimen, a soft smattering of hair across his mouth-watering pecs, his biceps enough to crush any resistance out of me. My god, what I could do with this man if he was really open to gay sex for pleasure instead of punishment.

He grabbed my throat and squeezed. "Shut the fuck up!" His face was over mine as he pumped savagely in and out of my asshole hitting my prostate often enough to have me swooning. I knew he was attempting to make it as painful as he could for me but then he slowed down, really getting off on the feeling of fucking me. "Holy shit! This is the best ass I've ever fucked. If I wasn't straight I'd marry the fag just for his ass. I bet his throat is just as sweet. Logan, get up here on the couch and fuck his face."

It took a bit of maneuvering but eventually Logan managed to stand over me and lower his cock into my mouth. "I'm next," Marty said as if afraid he'd miss out. If Colt seemed to be a connoisseur of sex, Logan was his antithesis. My mouth was merely a receptacle for his cock and then as fast as possible, his sperm. He was fucking my face at an odd angle, stabbing my palate and my throat with his sizeable cock, choking me, making me gag.

"Dude, if you take it slower and not like a bull at a gate, you'll enjoy it more," Colt suggested, pulling his cock out of my ass. "I can't do it like this. Looking at your scrawny ass, Logan, while I'm fucking the fag is just not doing it for me. Here, get off him for a minute."

Logan withdrew and slumped off the couch allowing me to catch my breath, my chin covered with mucous from the pummeling I'd endured.

Colt looked me over. "If you promise to be a good boy we can make you more comfortable and we can all enjoy ourselves." I was up for that, although I'd have to make a break for it as soon as I could. "Promise you won't try to escape?"

Coughing as if to get the taste of Logan out of my throat, I nodded consent.

"Help him out of those ankle straps, then we can do him doggy fashion and you guys won't have to look at his faggy face." That might have suited the others but I had the feeling Colt liked the look of my sweet femme features. I wasn't about to call him on it.

They manhandled me off the lounge and onto the floor. I was wobbly on my feet at first having been in the spread-eagled position for a longer period of time than normal. Once I'd regained my balance I made a half-hearted break for it, more for show than anything else, but I didn't get far before Logan tripped me up. None of the others, bar Colt of course, seemed perturbed that I might get away. So far they hadn't really become physically involved.

Logan hauled me to my feet. "Don't try that again, pretty boy, or I will really will shove my fist up your back passage and ruin you for good."

I did wonder who he'd practiced on.

"Marty, clear the coffee table. I've got an idea." Marty, ever obedient, had the snacks and alcohol moved to the dining nook at the speed of lightning so eager did he seem to get his turn at my mouth. Colt grabbed some cushions from the couch and placing them on the coffee table commanded me to kneel on them with my ass vulnerable at one end and my mouth at the other as I bent forward. I was at cock height so no-one would have to stoop.

"You take his mouth Marty. And you can have his ass for a while, Ken. I don't want to ruin him for the rest of you." Colt was dictating who did what to me. I heard a couple of whispered gripes.

"Um, if it's all the same to you, Colt, I'd rather just, ah, get a blow job. Fucking his ass just seems a bit too gay to me."

"You suggesting something, eh Ken?" Colt asked.

"No, no, don't get me wrong. I don't fuck chicks in the ass either so…" he shrugged.

"I'll tag his ass, Colt. Marty can have his mouth." Dil sounded confident but then spoiled the effect by adding, "It won't turn me gay will it if I like it?"

"I'm loving the feel of his ass squeezing my cock, you think I've turned gay?" Colt glared, defying him to say it had.

Dil was already stroking his cock to erection. "Hell no, you're the bluest blooded hetero I've ever met." He moved it to my mouth. "Slick it up, fag. Get it nice and moist before I stick it in your ass." I didn't have to be asked twice and slobbered all over his shaft, licking his piss slit, wishing I could have my way with his balls. But as soon as he was hard enough he moved behind me and without fanfare prodded his cock against my asshole and pushed. I saw stars for a moment before he got himself positioned comfortably. "Fuck, you're not wrong, mate, that is one sweet ass."

I felt every inch of him as he pounded into me, unfortunately missing my prostate at every stroke but still filling me with hot hard cock. Only problem was – my mouth was empty.

"For fuck's sake, Marty, get over there and fuck his face. We haven't got all day," Colt sounded impatient. Perhaps he expected Brad home soon.

Marty poked his cock in my face tentatively. I stuck my tongue out to lick the head and he shuddered. He was obviously unused to anyone putting their mouth round his long thick cock. My mouth watered at the sight but he was so tentative my tongue barely touched it. "Come on, Marty, put it in my mouth. I'm gagging for it!" I moaned in frustration.

No sooner spoken than done, aided somewhat by Colt steering Marty into me. I would have thanked him if my mouth hadn't been full, so I acknowledged his help with a quirk of my eyebrows. Marty gasped, Marty panted, Marty shuddered, and Marty blew his wad in almost record time he was so excited. After I'd sucked out every spoonful of his sweet jizz, I licked his prick clean but he pulled out of my mouth quickly he was so sensitive, quickly zipping up and moving aside, mumbling, "He's all yours, Ken."

Ken was the most reluctant of all of them to be physically involved so when he pushed his cock in my face it was almost completely limp. I licked the underside, I sucked the knob, I did everything from my bag of tricks but he remained resolutely uninterested. I thought of sucking his dick into my mouth as was and pretending he'd blown a load, thus relieving him of any embarrassment. Sometimes guys who can't perform became violent. I had one last trick. I reached out and pulled him forward, holding his dick aloft as I headed for his balls. He was stunned. I guess he'd never thought of his testicles as an erogenous zone before. He did now. "Holy fuck. Where did you learn to do that?" His cock, obviously upset at missing out, suddenly stiffened and beat against my face to gain attention. I turned my expertise to his shaft after giving his balls a good workout, swallowing it whole. Okay, that was showing off but he was loving it. He held the back of my head and started to thrust gracelessly.

Dil, pounding my ass as if he'd never fuck again in this lifetime, jerked my body forward to choke on Ken's cock with every thrust. I was in hog heaven.

Eventually Ken let out a wail like a horny banshee and I felt his spunk squirt into the back of my throat. Holding my head tight against him until his balls emptied, he stumbled as he pulled out of my mouth, sitting heavily in an armchair, his slimy cock hanging limp from the fly of his trousers.

Dil filled the silence with profanities. "Fuckin' fag scum, take my cock. I'm gonna fuck you till you pass out, you fucker." I heartily approved of his verbal dexterity. There's nothing more cum invigorating than good porn dialogue and Dil seemed a master of it. "I'm gonna fill your ass with my hot spunk. Fill you till you overflow, then wipe my cock on your fag face. How do ya like the sound of that, cunt?"

I would have told him I liked the sound of that just fine but Colt decided it was time he had a taste of my mouth action. He was a big boy and I felt it touch the sides all the way down my throat, my face impaled on his prick until I thought I'd choke and pass out. He let me go at the last moment and I gasped for air, mucous running down my chin, my eyes watering like they'd never stop.

"I like how you look, boy," Colt said gazing down at me. "All fucked out. But I bet you still want more, don't you?"

I coughed to clear my throat. "Bet your sweet ass, I want more. I want cock in my ass until I can't sit down for leaking man slime."

"You'll get your wish, fag boy. We'll rip you a new asshole. Fill you with spunk until you beg us to stop. Fill your stomach with our spooge. You think it's gonna be over tonight, well think again. When Brad dumps your sorry ass we'll be waiting, boy. You're gonna be our cum dump, our sex boy toy. You'll do everything we want. If Logan wants to shove his fist up your ass, you'll beg him for it. Got that?"

I nodded because I was still trying to get my breath back.

"Can't hear you," Colt said.

"Yes, sir," I bellowed as best I could.

In the background I heard a door open and close. For a moment I thought Brad was home but I realized when I heard Colt curse it was probably Ken and Marty sneaking out.

"Jesus Christ," Dil yelled and I felt his orgasm rocket into my ass. He must have been saving himself and I was the lucky recipient. He collapsed on my back until his breathing evened out then he yanked out his cock, spunk oozing down my leg.

"I'm off, guys. See you at work. Don't think it hasn't been. If you guys decide to keep this sweet fag ass on tap, let me know. I'll be there."

Three down, two to go. The two biggest bastards of the lot.

"Heads or tails," Colt asked.

"You've had both so I think I should get a turn at his ass first, then his throat. What do ya say?"

"I say let's get more comfortable." With that, Colt began removing his clothes. Fuck, he was fit. I wished Logan was within sight so I could see if he was the same. No matter, his cock was in my ass a few moments later.

"Come on, guys. Give it to me hard. I want to feel it. I want the smell of cum, the taste of cum, I want to drown in it."

"Maybe you will one day," Colt said. I thought I heard his brain hatching some sort of evil plan.

"Shit, you weren't wrong about his ass, Colt. This is super sweet. Badest fag ass I ever fucked. Yeah, you're right, mate, we gotta keep this on tap."

"Just you, me and Dil," Colt said, holding my nose until I opened my mouth to breathe before shoving his cock in to his balls. Luckily, I'd taken a good lungful of air and I took everything he gave me and silently begged for more.

Logan fucked like it was an Olympic sport, electrifying my body by hitting my prostate more often than I'd ever previously experienced. He and Colt kept up a steady flow of obscenities and fantasy about my future as their fuck toy until Colt unloaded in my mouth and Logan's cock spewed in my ass adding to the dumps that had gone before.

In the silence when they both paused for breath, I heard the front door open.

"What the fuck is going on here? What are you guys doing to my boyfriend?" Brad was home.

Colt decided on sarcasm. "If you can't tell what we're doing to your slut then you've been doing it wrong."

"He begged us for it," Logan said.

Brad looked at me. "Did they force themselves on you?"

I hung my head in shame. "Yeah."

"Fuckin' liar," Colt muttered. Then he stretched his body to full alpha height. "Doesn't really matter. Your career is as fucked as your boyfriend."

Brad smiled. Not the sort of smile you want to be on the receiving end of. I could see he was excited. His cock was straining against the fly of his trousers. He rubbed it through the material.

"Why don't you two sit and watch for a minute – I'm horny as fuck watching you two doing Samson over — and then we'll have ourselves a nice little discussion about how fucked you and your cronies are, Colt."

Colt snorted and went to grab his clothes from the floor. Brad kicked them out of his reach. "You too, Logan. Don't even think about leaving. I'll call the cops."

Sheepishly, they both sat naked on the lounge, attempting to hide their limp dicks.

"On Your back, slut," Brad commanded.

I slid on the coffee table and hoisted my legs in the air, my ass oozing the earlier deposit. Without any preliminaries, Brad unfastened his trousers, pulled them and his boxers down until he could step out of them and in a swift movement had his cock at my entrance and pushed. He slid in smoothly.

"Feels so hot inside," he said. "That must be your cum I can feel around my cock, Logan. Slimy man lube."

Unexpectedly Brad leaned over and kissed me full on the lips, licking Colt's residual cum from my mouth. "Mm, tasty." That seemed to spur him on to greater thrusts until he had me edging over and over again. His cock was bringing me to the greatest orgasm of my life.

"Come on, babe, now," he encouraged and cum shot out of my cock all over my chest and my stomach as I felt Brad deposit a load inside me.

He pulled out, stood and walked toward the duo on the lounge. "Now, let's talk turkey. Logan, suck my cock clean."

"Fuck off, loser."

"Colt?"

"I don't think so." He folded his arms across his chest and I noticed his cock was at half- mast.

"Okay, we can play it hard ball, if you like."

Colt got his courage back. "I'm getting dressed, walking out of here and on Monday at the office we'll see your ass fired so fast you won't know what hit you."

Logan took that as his signal to reach for his clothes.

"I really wouldn't if I were you, Logan. Or you either, Colt." There was something cold and authoritative in his voice that made them both pause. He barely raised his voice when he said. "Now sit the fuck down!"

They were so surprised they did as instructed.

"We're going to have a little chat. I'll get around to your accomplices over the weekend. They're small beer, you two are what interests me."

"Can we cut to the chase, I've got a home to get back to," Colt bluffed.

Brad was ominous. "Maybe not for much longer. A home to get back to I mean. Not if I tell your families what you two have been up to."

Colt snorted. Logan looked ill.

"Like anyone would believe you after we tell them about your slut here."

"Well, unlike you, Colt, I have footage to back up my argument."

"Footage?" Logan stuttered.

"You see, I didn't need to head kilometers out of my way to pick up beer for a party. The garage has quite a few slabs so all I had to do was grab a couple and bring them inside. Imagine my surprise when I see my work mates forcing themselves on my boyfriend. I had my phone with me so I thought I should film what was happening for posterity because it sure looked like you were forcing poor Sam here to do things he really didn't want to. Am I right, babe?"

I kept a straight face. "Oh, yeah."

"You won't show my wife, will you?" Logan was practically begging.

"Well, you did refuse to clean my cock with your tongue…"

Logan was on his knees crawling toward Brad quicker than a streak of lightning.

"Get back on the lounge, Logan. You had your chance."

"So, what is it you want?" Colt asked. He was ready to negotiate.

"You're a sensible man, Colt. And you look horny as fuck ploughing your cock in my boyfriend. I think I'd like to see that a bit more often."

I stared at Brad. He winked. I mouthed, "You bastard." He'd set the whole thing up.

"Did you enjoy the guys fucking you, babe," Brad asked. "The truth."

"I fucking loved it!"

"Mm, I thought you might. Wanna do it again?"

"Hell, yeah."

"Good." Brad turned to the two on the lounge. "Here's how it's gonna be. You, Colt, will go see your uncle over the weekend and tell him you think your skills are better suited to another area of the company. Human Resources. Advertising and Promotion. Anywhere but the position you're in now. You will tell him what a great job I did on the new account and tell him I'm the perfect person to take your place. If he hesitates, you'll tell him I've had offers elsewhere and I will take some of the contracts with me. Got it?"

"So far. Never liked that department anyway." I could see Colt was intrigued, probably waiting for the punishments.

"You will also inform management that you have found the ideal person to manage the staff gym. You will convince them they need an onsite manager who can help with equipment maintenance, take classes in aerobics and what not, and generally keep the staff in shape. That person will be Sam. Understood?"

WTF? I'd been looking for a permanent position for months.

Colt sneered, obviously uncomfortable that he wasn't in control. "Anything else?"

"Oh, yes. Now comes the best part." Colt and Logan flinched at the prospect. "You will both continue to fuck Sam on a regular basis, either at the company gym or here at our home. I will be in attendance to watch. I've discovered that watching Sam fucked senseless by other men gets me horny as fuck. Sometimes I'll join in, sometimes I'll just watch."

"You want us to fuck your boyfriend? Are you serious?" Colt sounded flabbergasted.

"Uh huh. We got a deal?"

"Hell, yeah. I'll fuck Sam's hot ass every chance I get."

"Logan?"

He had a look of utter disbelief on his face. "You're not gonna tell my wife?"

"Not if you agree to keep fucking my boyfriend."

"That's it? No hard feelings, no repercussions over what we did tonight."

"Nah. Speaking for myself, I enjoyed every moment of watching my own live porn show. Took a lot of self-control not to join in earlier. And I'm pretty sure Sam loved it too."

I tried not to make my nod of agreement too enthusiastic.

SOLD BY MY STEPDAD

My stepdad's never been very supportive of me. My mom remarried after my dad headed for pastures greener and never came back. My new dad has never liked me even more so when my mom finally succumbed to the cancer that was eating away at her insides. Up until then she'd been a protective barrier between her new husband's ire and me. His hatred of me has only grown since her passing.

Deke, my younger stepbrother is favorite because he's a chip off the old block, a blood son, a younger version of the old man, right down to the arrogant asshole personality. Conversely, I'm a bit on the 'soft' side. I'm not gay if that's what you're thinking, although I have experimented a little. I don't know what I am...probably too timid for either gender.

My major is Costume Design, adding to the ridicule. Deke constantly repeats, "Ooh, that'll get you a good job in the big, wide world of real life." Like he'd know about the big wide world...he's a corporate raider, for crying out loud. He walked straight out of high school into a job at his dad's firm.

He might be right though. Problem is I don't know whether I am cut out for real life. That's precisely why my stepdad—I could never bring myself to call him 'dad' even though my mom told me it would help our relationship and make life easier for her— decided I needed toughening up. It galled me to even call him Karl. He was of the opinion I should join a gym to build up my body. For 'body' read 'masculinity.' And not just any gym, the gym that his company part owns and where Deke works out. I lasted exactly three visits, after which no amount of threats, cajoling or blackmail would get me back through the doors. I likened the gym to a medieval torture chamber.

Karl let my easy capitulation rest for a while, although it was another black mark against my masculinity, or lack thereof. I could read what a letdown I was in his eyes like a headline in the morning newspaper. My brother took every opportunity to ridicule my manhood, stopping just short of calling me a faggot, although I know he wanted to.

When we argued bitterly over the family's dubious and ruthless business practices, it wasn't long before he did finally use the F word. "I'm not a faggot!" I yelled in response.

"Of course not, Brady," he sneered, grabbing a handful of his crotch. "Faggots are at least useful for something."

Karl snickered, not an ounce of reprimand in his face. He beamed his approval at what Deke had said and done. Sighing, he turned to me, "If you won't man up at the gym, I don't know what we're gonna do with you."

Strangely enough, I did like working out. It made me feel good about myself. I just didn't like Karl's gym, which treated its customers as if they were trainees in boot camp. If I'd wanted that sort of regimented instruction, I would have joined the Army. As there's not a militaristic bone in my body I joined a more down-market establishment where the approach was sufficiently hands-on to get me started before I was left to progress at my own pace.

Knowing neither Karl nor Deke would approve, I tried to keep my burgeoning new body hidden beneath layers of loose-fitting clothing. Soon, however, my brother noticed. He was startled by the change in me. Not in my personality, but in my body mass and musculature. I had definition. I found I had a small number of admirers who wanted to do things to my dick. Some were scared off by my inexperience, but a handful siphoned off all my ball juice while I sat passively. I never reciprocated. They muttered their thanks or admiration for my 'big cock.' I'd never thought of it as anything more than average—like the rest of me—but then I had nothing against which to compare it. I began looking when I was in the showers, which got me the wrong sort of reputation.

I kept my new body hidden because my father would expect that I would 'man up' in direct proportion to my new 'manly' physique. Inside, however, I was still the same mousy personality regardless of how good I looked. My brother's reaction was about what I expected. Jealousy. Worse still, now he felt he could use the F-word more freely in front of his dad. Suspicious of my new body shape, one day he flipped my sweatshirt over my head to reveal that my pecs, abs and biceps were now large enough to have an IQ of their own. After his initial surprise at that unveiling, he'd yanked down my track pants to reveal my tight fashion underpants that all but thrust my cock and balls into any onlooker's line of sight and hugged my ass so tightly they threatened to disappear up my ass crack.

That seemed to confirm everything for my brother. His face turned up in derision. "You may have got your body all pumped up, but it just makes you look even more like a faggot."

Karl and Deke had dark hair and coloring whereas I'd taken after mom who was blonde and blue-eyed. As an added taunt, I'd allowed my hair to grow longer than my stepdad decreed acceptable. His only comment was "You look like a girl." Still, I knew what he really meant. After my brother had stripped me practically naked, Karl looked me over and his nostrils flared as if he'd been confronted with a bad smell. "Cover yourself up, you look ridiculous."

No further mention was made of my new and improved body as Karl saw no accompanying improvement whatsoever in my social skills. In some respects, I would have done anything to be like my Karl and Deke. I wanted the same easy extroverted personality that enabled them to function so successfully in the real world. I wanted their confident, swaggering sexuality. Hell, I just wanted to be good at something, anything. No such luck. Small, niggling incidents fanned the flame of Karl's disappointment, the last being when three young skateboarders humiliated me in the street in full view of our neighbors.

He watched the episode unfold. They had blocked the entrance to our front gate, denying me access. I tried reasoning. I tried bribery. I knew curtains had been pulled aside so the neighbors were witness to my humiliation, but no one ventured out to help me. Bastards. Those kids had been intimidating the whole neighborhood for the past five months, vandalizing private property, stealing from mailboxes, and generally making nuisances of themselves. I even tried begging them to let me pass until Karl, so embarrassed by the fact he was forced to intervene, flattened the little bastards. "What the fuck is the matter with you?" he screamed once we'd gone inside to the comparative privacy of our own home.

"There's nothing the matter with me," I said defensively. "There were three of them."

"They're just fuckin' kids. A good fart would have blown them away."

He made it look so easy. He's a big man with a big personality, a mountain of testosterone, whereas I'm a seething mass of indecisiveness. I'm not a coward exactly, but I'm no hero either. Nor do I want to be. I'd be happy just to be less fearful. I didn't dare tell him that while those kids humiliated me in the street, my cock was hard as concrete.

He sighed. "You've got to grab life by the balls or people will eat you up and spit you out." I did admire the way Karl faced life head on, ready for any emergency, fearless and determined. He was basically the sort of man I admired. I just didn't like the way he conducted his business. It broke my heart to see the resignation in his eyes that I would never amount to anything he would consider worth his time and effort.

As a punishment for my cowardice, he insisted I remain home the next day to liaise with the builders he had engaged to renovate and paint a spare room. They had proven difficult and lazy. A confrontation would prove, or disprove, my manliness once and for all times.

The new room was special because it would become his home office and allow him to conduct business at any hour of the day or night. If I fucked up…

"I can't do it myself because I have a meeting with the most important client of my career, a big new corporate fish. I want to impress him. He's worth millions to the company and I intend to hook him."

I looked duly impressed even though I wasn't. Anticipating my next question, he added, "And your brother has to sit in on a scheduled Board meeting in my place."

Mumbling about assignments and missing classes as an excuse to avoid the task which had Major Conflict written all over it, I knew it would do no good. I didn't want to stay home because I'm a klutz around people I'm supposed to supervise, and these guys sounded like a real case. "You'll have to crack the whip because they're being paid by the hour, so they'll attempt to work as slowly as possible. Milk the clock, you understand," Karl said.

Great. Just what I needed. He couldn't just pay them for the finished job and let it go at that. He was always a tight bastard, wanting his pound of flesh. I guess that's why he's wealthy and I live in a big house with all the modern conveniences and drive to college, unlike the other poor bastards who have to work at burger joints in a vain attempt to pay for the tuition and books, with little left over for necessities such as food and accommodation.

Karl woke me early—to him any man with the determination to succeed rose early enough to beat his competition. It seems I would never be top of my game because I loved sleeping until seven or eight o'clock. I had no corporate throats to cut so I slept easy. My stepdad sighed when he saw the outfit I'd chosen to meet the builders: all color coordinated in pastel shades. I thought it looked smart and screamed good taste; he merely thought it screamed.

He sent me back to change, swearing vehemently about my intransigence, even going so far as to use the F-word because my provocative behavior was making him late. Provocative? I'd give him fuckin' provocative. I changed into my tightest pair of cut-off jeans that I never wore in public as they left no doubt at all that I'd been circumcised at birth. They threatened to strangle my balls and clung to my ass crack like glue so that I'm sure if I bent over you'd see an outline of my butt hole. The bottom of my ass cheeks could not be contained in the flimsy material and jutted from the rough hem of the seat. I wore a clingy T-shirt, two sizes too small, that threatened to rip apart every time I flexed a muscle. They also showed off my hard pecs and their pert little nipples that, if I'd had time, I would have had pierced as one final 'fuck you' to the family who found any sort of body modification repellent. When I stormed out of my bedroom to confront my stepdad, I shouted, "If you want to see faggot, then get a load of this." It seems somewhere in my time at the gym I'd grown a pair. I was giddy with bravado.

Obviously, Karl had got sick of waiting and headed off to his important meeting while I'd been busy choosing my outfit. I'd probably been too angry to hear his shouted goodbyes—if he'd even bothered. What I hadn't counted on was the builders having their own key for they'd let themselves into the house and were standing in the doorway gaping at my getup, smirking like a gang of adolescents. To cover my embarrassment, I merely looked at my watch.

Tony, the foreman, a good-looking Italian in his forties, around the same age as my stepdad but with a bit of a beer gut, dropped his tools where he stood. "Don't fuckin' start. I've just had your old man on the cell phone bawling me out for being late.

I don't have to put up with shit like that. And I won't put up with it from a snotty-nosed brat like you. Understand?"

I didn't care as long as he got the job done and didn't slack off while they were at it. "I'll be keeping an eye on you," I said, realizing my mistake as soon as the words were out of my mouth. The guys all laughed. Two of them, both swarthy men in their early-to-mid thirties, were built like brick shithouses, their muscles bulging through their overalls. The youngest was an apprentice in his early twenties with long surf-bleached hair: he was an Aussie and wore shorts and no top. He was well muscled, though not as thickly as the others. I thought it wise to watch them set up as they were on the clock.

There was a certain amount of horsing around, attempts to grab one another's crotch and generally telling each other to "suck this" or "kiss my ass" while they grabbed a handful of crotch or butt. I let them have their fun at my expense, Karl's expense, without comment before I disappeared upstairs to my bedroom to work on an essay that was due shortly. For the first hour or so they worked steadily, although they were accompanied by a radio turned up way too loudly for me to study effectively. In exasperation, I finally went downstairs to ask if they could turn it down because I couldn't concentrate.

"Concentrate on what?" Tony smirked. "Internet porn?" He winked at his workers. "I bet you're up there jerking your cock."

I went red. "I certainly am not." My indignation did not have the force I'd hoped as I stuttered.

"By the way you're dressed I'd say you're jerking off looking at other guys' cocks."

I went even redder. "Fuck off!" I stormed back to my room and slammed the door. I was about to pick up the phone and call

Karl before I thought better of it. That was exactly what he would be expecting. He certainly wouldn't want to be interrupted when he was with a major client. I calmed down and went back to work as best I could under the difficult circumstances. An hour later Karl called to check on the progress. I lied and told him everything was going well. He didn't sound convinced.

"Don't take any shit from them. They're working for me. I'm paying them good money. So stand up to them if you have to." He'd already disconnected the call before I could ask him how his day was going. Typical. I went back downstairs, determined the workmen wouldn't embarrass me this time. When I got to the bottom of the stairs, Kareem, one of the dark-skinned men, whistled and grabbed a handful of his cock through his overalls. "Look, he's blushing like a virgin," he yelled.

"Bet he's anything but a virgin," Ali laughed. "You see the way he's been looking at my crotch."

"I have not!" I yelled. "Anyway, my stepdad just rang and he wants to see results when he gets back, otherwise…"

"Otherwise what?" Tony said ominously.

"Just otherwise," I mumbled.

"Coffee break," yelled Ali.

In unison, the guys all dropped their tools.

"Hey," I shouted weakly. "You've hardly even started."

"Yeah," said Ali, "but unless we get taken care of every few hours, we get sort of stressed and our work suffers."

"You wouldn't want that, would you?" smirked Tony. "What will Daddy say if he gets home and finds the work's not up to his standards?"

"He won't be happy," I mumbled.

"And what does he do when he's not happy?" Tony asked.

"He yells at…" and I stopped a little too late. They all burst out laughing.

"Hey, Jack," Ali called to the Aussie kid, "come and get it," and he unclipped his overalls and flopped out a huge semi-hard cock that he started to milk. Jack ambled over and sank to his knees, engulfing the cock in one mouthful. Ali held the back of his head and face-fucked him until gag and drool started to ooze over Jack's chin.

"Stop it!" I yelled. "My stepdad doesn't like faggots."

"Oh, you mean like Jack there?"

"Yeah," I replied, wishing I'd kept my mouth shut.

"You never jerked off with your buddies?" Ali asked.

"Yeah," I admitted reluctantly.

"Well, that's faggot stuff," Tony said.

"But I don't put it in my mouth," I responded quickly so they wouldn't get the wrong idea. That's not to say Ali's cock didn't look mouthwatering. I must have been drooling while I stared at the scene.

Tony leered. "Put your tongue away, boy. I'm sure Ali will give you a go if you ask politely. Won't you, mate?"

"I love nothing more than a young college boy down on his knees worshipping my Persian cock," he replied, waving his dick toward me.

During the brief conversation, Jack had slipped off his shorts. His butt was like sun-kissed marble and his cock, already leaking pre-cum, was large and long nestled in a tuft of blond pubes. He bent over in front of me and Tony pulled his ass cheeks apart. "He's got the most perfect asshole in the world."

Ali snickered.

"We fuck him," said Kareem. Hauling out his own slab of circumcised meat, he spat in his hand, lubricated his prick and rammed it in Jack's willing ass. At the same time, Ali lined his cock up with Jack's mouth and gagged him. I couldn't believe Jack's tiny asshole could take a cock the size of Kareem's or that Ali's wasn't suffocating him. Tony peeled off his own clothes; he had a chest almost as good as my stepdad's but with clumps of black hair stretching down to his cock.

Karl was shaved all over. He told me women find it sexy when a man is as smooth as a billiard ball, plus it makes his cock look bigger. I spied on him once while he jacked off, and I'd jerked my cock to that image for months after.

Tony put his naked arm around me while stroking his cock with his other hand. "You want a go at Jack's ass, son?" he asked me. I didn't want Jack's ass, but Ali and Kareem's cocks... I couldn't take my eyes off them. "No! My stepdad would kill me if he ever knew I did that sort of thing."

"I bet he wouldn't be able to resist Jack's boy pussy," Kareem grunted. "Or his cunt mouth."

"My stepdad's not a faggot," I yelled and shucked Tony's arm off my shoulder.

"Have it your own way, son," Tony said. "Dressed like that, we thought you were a player."

"Well you thought wrong!" This morning was not going well. "You guys are sick," I muttered as I headed back up the stairs to my room. My concentration was shot even though I tried my darnedest to get back to my college essay. Visions of Ali's cock and Jack's mouth closing over it kept intruding. My own cock was a traitor, staying resolutely hard no matter what I thought about. I was confused. Was it because I wanted Ali's cock or Jack's mouth? Perhaps a bit of both. Shit, why did my stepdad throw me in the deep end like this? Unless…

It suddenly occurred to me that this was a test. Perhaps Karl knew what these guys were like and wanted to test whether I was a faggot after all. I seethed for half an hour, which drove the sexual escapades I'd witnessed downstairs out of my head. As my anger dissipated, I thought it was a mean trick to play—if that was his intention. Still, I couldn't believe he was that venal. After all, he had demanded I change my outfit before the builders arrived.

My thoughts were interrupted by a knock at the door. I swung around in my desk chair to confront Tony, who was leaning against the frame. "Just to let you know, we've had to turn off the water downstairs to the kitchen and the bathroom so the guys may have to come upstairs to use the…uh…facilities from time to time."

"My parents' room is out of bounds so you'll have to use my bathroom," I said, nodding toward the door on the other side of the bed. Tony walked over to the en suite and, without closing the door, unzipped and hauled out his cock. I watched out of the corner of my eye so as not to appear too interested. He pissed loudly into the bowl, shook his prick to dislodge the last drops, squeezing his foreskin over the head, before he flushed. Rather than zip his trousers back up again, he slowly began to milk his cock. I was so shocked, I gave myself away.

"What are you doing?"

"If you have to ask because you can't see, then perhaps you should come closer." "Certainly not," I snorted.

"In that case, I'll come over and show you."

Without releasing his cock and before I could tell him not to bother, he stepped out of the bathroom and up where I sat at my desk. He continued to stroke his dick, which was getting wet and shiny around the slit. He scooped some of the leakage onto his finger and offered it to me. I turned my face away. I was both fascinated and repulsed by what he wanted me to do.

"Lick it off," he commanded in a voice that brooked no argument. I was so surprised that he would speak to the son of the man who was paying his wages in such a disrespectful manner.

"No way," I said, but my voice was hoarse, whether with desire or fear I wasn't sure. He laughed.

"I think you will," he said. "And a lot more. You'll like it too."

"I don't think so," I said with less confidence than before.

Tony grabbed a handful of my hair, yanking my head back. I cried out in pain and while my mouth was open he shoved his slimy finger roughly into my mouth. "Don't even think about biting me," he sneered, "or you'll find yourself scalped." For emphasis, he pulled my hair tighter, making me wince in pain. "Lick it."

I had never tasted another man before. In fact, I had never tasted myself.

The sweet and slightly salty flavor came as a surprise and was not as unpleasant as I'd expected. When I blocked from my mind what I was swallowing and from whence it came, it was actually very exciting.

"Good boy," he said, releasing my hair and patting me on the top of my head. "That wasn't so bad, was it?"

"No, sir," I mumbled. He must have picked up on my use of the word 'sir' for he immediately asked, "Is that what you like, boy? A big, strong man to tell you what to do? To treat you rough?"

Even though it felt like he was patronizing me, I answered truthfully. "I don't know, sir. I've never had anyone treat me that way." My eyes were downcast, looking at his cock. I thought he would scoop more of his pre-cum onto his finger and feed me, but instead he held the back of my head to guide my face toward his cock. Attempting to pull back, I panicked. "I can't, sir. I've never done that before." He showed no anger at my reluctance, holding my head still, a matter of inches from his throbbing cock. "I bet you want to, though. Don't you?"

I amazed myself by nodding. "Go ahead then," he encouraged. "Kiss it." Blocking the mental sound of my stepdad's voice and his rants on the evils of faggotry, I leaned forward to lick the weeping head of Tony's cock, trembling as I tasted still more of his masculinity. Soon, I'd licked him clean. Refusing to think, I opened my lips and took Tony's prick into my mouth. I was familiar enough with the basics.

Tony guided me further along the path to good cock-sucking technique, informing me when my teeth were not shielded enough by his painful intake of breath, urging me to use my tongue, suggesting I take a break from time to time to work on his balls, until I was feeling quite the expert. He heaped praise on my ability for a beginner.

The drought of affection and encouragement from my own family was filled with Tony's praise. I realized I wanted to please him more than anything. Tony didn't rush things. I learned to relax and was enjoying my first foray into the world of dick munching. It was quite a discovery that the tongue can keep doing its job well after your mouth is stopped with hard, thick gristle; it doesn't have to just lie there inert.

Sure, the first time Tony's prick pushed into my throat, I panicked, but he withdrew quickly so I could gasp in breath. "You really are inexperienced, boy. But you learn fast." He patted me on the head. I took the move as praise, not as condescension.

Next time he ventured far enough into my gob, I was ready and accepted his cock into my throat. Not far and not for long, but enough to make Tony gasp. Then those words he spoke became music to my ears: "Son, you're a natural. You're really good at this." In my eagerness to impress, I tried too hard, attempting feats that probably only the most experienced could achieve without injury, but then cock sucking doesn't come with a warning: *Don't try this at home without expert instruction.*

My eyes teared up, snot ran out my nose and I coughed up mucous. "Take it easy, son," Tony said, more concern in his voice than I'd ever heard before. "It's not a competition. I'm not awarding gold medals here. I'm just trying to get my cock sucked. All I'm saying is, for a beginner you leave a lot of more experienced guys at the starting gate. Okay, you're not as good as young Jack downstairs, but with a bit more practice…" He left the statement open and it revealed a world of possibilities as he handed me a bunch of tissues from my desk to wipe my face.

When I'd finished, and had tossed them in the bin, Tony moved his cock back to my mouth. "Now, take it easy. Go at your own pace, but I gotta warn you, your mouth is so fuckin' hot and what you do with that tongue of yours has to be experienced to be believed… I'm gonna shoot in a matter of seconds rather than minutes. If you don't want to taste spunk then you best pull your face off my prick when I tell you to, otherwise you're gonna get so much ball juice down your throat the medics will have to pump your stomach."

I'd tasted a little of Tony's pre-cum—it was a bit like warm mucous—it didn't repulse me. But a full load? I didn't know if I'd barf. The mere idea of getting Tony's man essence inside me gave me a sort of thrill that almost had my cock squirting. Didn't matter what it tasted like, I was determined to keep it down. Of course, I would have loved to feel it spurt across my face or over my own cock, but I was hoping the home renovations would take a couple more days and that Tony might want to use my body again. And again. I was sold on this faggot shit my stepdad went on about. Maybe if he was wrong about that, perhaps he was wrong about what a no-hoper I was.

Time later to think about that, I had Tony's cock to concentrate on at that moment. I gave it everything I had, every trick in my very limited cock-sucking vocabulary, but Tony groaned his appreciation so I was doing something right. He did warn me as he promised so I could remove my mouth, but it just spurred me on to greater suction until Tony held my head, bucked, and moaned as he shot his load into my mouth. His cum was funky and rich. I swallowed it all without any side effects, licking my lips when Tony finally withdrew to squeeze the last few drops from his piss slit. I leaned over and licked him clean.

"You fuckin' swallowed the lot?" Tony said in amazement.

Now what was I supposed to do? I was still kneeling on the floor with my cock hard as concrete as Tony zipped up. I felt like an idiot to have been so vulnerable. I remained in position, expecting a barrage of insults to fall on my poor unfortunate head like raindrops in a summer shower.

"Come on, mate. Up on your feet," Tony said, helping me stand. He peeled my clothes off me until I was totally naked. I wondered what he had in mind. "I have a few lads that I think would be very grateful for your expertise."

He didn't sound as if he was being sarcastic. Still, I attempted to pull away from him but he held me tightly.

"Now, don't be like that. You and me both know you liked it. Hell, you more than liked it. You need a bit of experience and those lads downstairs are just the guys to give it to you."

I went with trepidation, Tony pulling at my arm as he dragged me along the hallway to the stairs. "You'll probably feel like a bit of a slut by the time we've finished with you," he said quietly, "but you'll thank us in years to come."

Because I hesitated, Tony picked me up and carried me down the stairs. Once at the bottom he put me down in all my naked glory, fixing me in place with his powerful arms. His ear-piercing whistle brought the other workers running although my naked body stopped them in their tracks. I didn't like the leers that curled the corners of their mouths. I felt like the fly in a sticky web of spiders. Tony offered me as if I was a virgin sacrifice. "Fresh meat, men."

Ali and Kareem licked their lips, while Jack settled for one word. "Wowee." The situation excited me so much my cock was already drooling. At the same time, the situation also frightened me. After all, these guys were big and rough-looking and nothing in their previous behavior led me to believe they'd go gentle on me. That made my heart beat faster.

I didn't want to get hurt, and I didn't know how far they would take this experience. I struggled and kicked in an effort to show I wasn't easy with the situation, but I was held tight.

"Don't fight it, mate," Tony whispered. "You'll only injure yourself. You want this as much as the guys want to give it to you."

Jack was the first to act. Kneeling in front of me, he went to work on my balls. He tugged on them firmly, licked my nuts, and then ran his tongue across the slit of my prick, causing me to gasp.

"He likes it." Kareem smiled.

"No, I don't," I protested weakly, but my traitorous oozing cock gave me away. Before I could protest further, Kareem leaned in and kissed me. I felt his powerful tongue force open my lips and he explored my mouth, demanding my surrender.

"Relax. Just go with it," Tony said, prodding my ass cheeks apart. He spat on his thick finger, then, after Kareem had finished his lip lock, pushed the finger into my mouth. "Grease it up good." Jack was chowing down on my full-masted cock, and the pleasure in my prick distracted me from Tony's explorations of my asshole. I almost didn't feel his finger push past my virgin ass entrance.

"Tight meat, men." Tony smiled as he pushed his finger farther into me. I tried to clench my ass to expel him, but it was no use. He flicked his big meaty finger about inside my butt until he hit the right button. I grunted and before I could stop, I unloaded into Jack's mouth. I didn't have time to warn him and apologized that I spunked in his mouth.

"That's the way I like it," he said, wiping his lips. "Down my throat and up my ass."

Two of Tony's fingers slid inside me so expertly I scarcely noticed because it felt so pleasurable. "He's a natural, men," he said as he removed his fingers, picking me up to carry me across to a makeshift work bench. He laid me on my back so Kareem could pull my legs apart and back over my head. It left my asshole exposed. I panicked when I realized what was going to happen, but before I could object, Kareem lowered his salty prick into my mouth to distract me.

I felt Tony slowly press his cock head, much bigger than two fingers, against my ass entrance. I saw stars even as I licked and sucked on Kareem's big black prick. This sure beat jerking off to Internet porn. I had a huge cock slowly pushing into my asshole and a Persian cock buried down my throat.

"Hey, Jack," Tony yelled. "This kid is good, really good. You better watch out or you might have competition."

Did he say I was good? That was the finest compliment I'd been paid in years. Okay, so it was about being a cock-sucking faggot who was having his asshole royally reamed, but...it was still a compliment.

"This kid is a pro," said Kareem. "I'd love to see his whole body covered in our spunk."

Ali and Jack watched as Kareem rammed his cock right down my throat up to his balls. "A natural slut." Jack smiled. "Like me." He leaned in to my ear and whispered, "You like cock, don't you, little bro?" I mumbled that I did. "You always wanted a big bro to play with, eh?" I nodded as best I could. "And how does it feel to have big prick in your asscunt, bro?" I nodded that I liked it. "Now you know why I love it every single day," he whispered. "Three big cocks ramming me every single day."

Jack stood up and Kareem made way for him. "Now suck my cock, boy." He rammed it so hard into my mouth I thought I'd be sick. He was reaming my throat, barely giving me time to breathe, while Tony was in my asshole ramming his big construction worker cock inside me. He pulled his prick out of my ass, and before I had time to adjust, he'd rammed it back inside me to the hilt. "I want to see your slut face," Tony said.

Jack pulled his cock out of my mouth so I could gasp for air allowing Tony to flip me over onto my back so I could watch his face as he rammed back inside me. "Ram my asshole. Harder," I cried out with more passion than I had ever felt before in my life. He didn't need to be asked twice, his cock battering inside so forcefully he knocked the wind out of me just as Jack pulled my face back on his prick. Ali leaned over and began to suck my salty cock that was standing up like a flagpole.

I was in heaven. Cock heaven. I knew I was just like Jack. I needed this, although I still had a lot to learn. Like how many cocks a slut can take in one day. I was concentrating on cock so much, Tony's in my ass and my big gay bro Jack's in my throat, I didn't hear the door open. It wasn't until a voice shouted, "What the fuck is going on here?" and I felt Tony's cock ripped out of my guts that I realized we'd been sprung. I looked up to see absolute disgust in my stepdad's eyes. If I hadn't been made stronger by Tony and his mates, I would have shriveled up inside and died. Further, I was surprised by the distinguished gent with Karl who looked amused rather than shocked. I noticed him adjust his crotch surreptitiously. The bulge in his fashionable expensive trousers held the promise of greatness.

"You sick fucks," Karl yelled, shoving Tony in the chest but barely moving him.

Tony was all reasonableness. "Calm down, man. We were just having a bit of fun."

"Fucking my son!" Now I was his son?

"Stepson," I mumbled, not helping the situation one bit.

Karl was purple with rage. "Turning him into a faggot. You call that fun?"

"No turning involved. He's a born cock slut," Jack said, not really helping calm the situation and more than I did. My stepdad spluttered with anger and went for Jack, but Tony easily waylaid him.

"Cool down," he said. "You're scaring your boy."

It was true, fearing what would happen to me after the workers left.

"Get your gear and clear out," Karl yelled. "If I ever see you anywhere near here again then I'll have the cops on you."

"Nothing we did was illegal. And it was all consensual." Tony put a strong arm around my stepdad's shoulder, effectively trapping him. "My men and I really like this job. We'll finish it and we'll even give you buddy rates. Bit of a discount."

"I'm not a prostitute," I muttered indignantly.

Karl ignored me like I didn't matter. "That doesn't alter the fact you were fucking my son."

The stranger, who had remained quiet up to this point, decided he'd add his tuppence worth. "Looked to me like he was thoroughly enjoying himself."

Tony was quick to agree, "That he was."

"He was looking for a bit of affection, mate," Jack added. "You ever compliment him? Ever tell him how good he is at anything?"

"Of course," Karl said, but I could see he knew it was a lie. "I've been busy. Business takes up most of my waking hours. I haven't always been able to devote the time to him I should." That must have reminded him that he had someone with him he was attempting to impress mightily. He groaned. "Oh, shit. What must you think of this fucked-up mess?"

"Great abs," said the stranger. "He must work out a lot."

"His pecs are almost bigger than Dolly Parton's." Jack gave them a squeeze. "Close your eyes and he's almost as pretty as a girl."

"But he's not a girl," Karl snapped.

"He sucks better than a girl," Tony replied. "Bet you love getting your dick sucked, eh? Good-looking guy like you must have chicks lining up to blow you."

"Not as much as I'd like," Karl admitted.

"Jack'd be glad to help you out, wouldn't you, Jack?" Kareem said. Karl shook his head vehemently. "No way! I don't do faggot shit!"

"Maybe you'd like that little cocksucker of a stepson of yours to suck your cock," Tony suggested.

"Fuck off!" Karl struggled to get free.

"What about you, mate?" Tony asked the stranger.

"If he's as good as you say he is, I'd choke the little fucker on my cock every chance I had."

My stepdad was shocked. "What sort of man are you, Sturgess?"

"Not one to look an opportunity in the face and not take it," he sneered. "I thought you were a man who played on the edge, Karl. Who grabbed every opportunity with both hands. Who took no prisoners."

"We're talking about my fuckin' useless stepson here, Sturgess."

"Useless? Not from what I've seen."

I was being discussed like I was a slab of meat on a butcher's block. I should have been upset, especially by the belittling remarks my old man made, but I was too turned on by the fact there were a number of men who found me attractive and my skills, no matter how newly acquired, worthwhile. Tony gripped Karl hard.

"Kareem! Ali! Show this big strong businessman what his son is really like." The men moved in, and I could see my stepdad was ready to attack them. Kareem parted my ass cheeks while Ali pulled my legs over my head. Sturgess and my stepdad were looking straight at my asshole. "Look at that," Tony teased as Kareem pushed his big thick black finger into my tight hole. "Look what your little boy likes," teased Jack. It was almost a whisper. Hypnotic.

Kareem removed his finger and planted his cock head at the entrance to my ass. Then he sank his cock up to the pubes. I groaned and Karl just stared, openmouthed. Ali positioned himself to sink his cock into my throat, sliding in and out. "He's such a good fuck," said Jack seductively. "Your stepson loves tough man cock. We're gonna give it to him while you watch."

Karl attempted unsuccessfully to wrench free of Tony's grip. Kareem started to work over my ass so that my eyes rolled back in my head at each stroke. He was fucking me like I hoped to be fucked for evermore while Ali's cock throbbed in my mouth. I wanted to taste his load. "Give me your fuckin' cum, men," I begged.

I'd never used language like that before. I didn't care anymore. I didn't give a fuck what happened after this day was over, all I knew was my future involved cock. Lots of cock.

Ali held my head as he worked his prick down my throat, thrusting a few times until he couldn't control himself any longer and then grunted. I felt his cum spurt into my mouth. After a few late spasms, he pulled out.

"Look, stepdaddy," Jack said as he held my face, showing my lips and tongue covered in gag and slimy cum. "This mouth was made for cock." He plopped his own cock in my mouth, gently fucking my well-lubed throat.

"You like?" Tony asked Sturgess.

"He likes," grinned Ali, pointing to the bulge in Sturgess's trousers.

"Maybe he wants a piece of choice stepson-cunt," Jack suggested. Kareem groaned loudly as I felt his cock pulse, shooting streams of spunk deep inside me. He shuddered for a moment, then regained control and pulled out. Ali spread my legs so my fucked hole was there for all to see. Sturgess unzipped and hauled out his meat. It was thick and heavily veined. It was also leaking shiny pre-cum.

"What the fuck are you doing?" my stepdad shouted.

"When it comes to getting what I want, I'm ruthless. Whether it's business or life. I thought you were a guy after my own heart. Obviously, I was wrong. And if I'm wrong, there's no sense in us doing business." Sturgess spat in his hand and greased his cock.

My ass was already well dilated by the cocks I'd had inside me earlier, well lubricated from their spunk. Still, his cock looked more than a match for my ass. I didn't care how much it hurt, I wanted it inside me. Sturgess aimed his weapon and pushed. I shuddered as it entered me in one thrust, burning my ass muscles as it slid inside, stretching me wide open. His balls smacked against my ass cheeks. Considerately, he remained still for a moment, allowing me to get used to the feeling. When I'd relaxed, and was sure I could take the monster, I begged, "Fuck me, Sturgess. Fuck me hard. Show me how much you love my ass."

"Oh, I will, son. I'll fuck your hole until you can't stand up. I'll fill you with all my spunk until it's running out your nostrils. You're so fuckin' tight." To my surprise, Sturgess leaned over me and crushed his mouth against mine. I couldn't believe he was kissing me, forcing his tongue between my lips and my teeth. I gasped for breath as he spread my legs wide to enter me even deeper than he had already, his weight crushing me against the workbench.

I was the center of the universe at this moment and I loved it. All the attention was focused on me. No one was bagging me now. They liked me. They were showing me in the best possible way. My one regret was that my stepdad couldn't bring himself to like me as well. Sturgess roared as I got my hands into the front of his shirt, buttons popping, and pinched his erect nipples hard.

"Oh fuck!" he screamed. "What I wouldn't give to have this on tap twenty-four/seven. I've been looking for someone like you all my life."

Then my stepdad spoke. And broke my heart. "What exactly would you give?"

Everything in the room stopped. Sturgess ceased his pounding mid-stroke. He turned to look at my father, a smile spreading across his face. He pulled his cock out of my ass, standing to confront my stepdad. "You're serious, aren't you?"

Neither man looked at me. Karl shrugged. "Wasn't it you that said you'll do whatever it takes to get what you want?"

"Close enough," Sturgess admitted.

"So will I. You want that faggot on tap?"

Sturgess glanced back at me spread out on the bench, my ass dripping. "Why not?"

"What have you got to trade?" Karl enquired, a shark-like grin on his face. He'd obviously found a way to rid himself of an unwanted faggot stepson and make profit from it.

Sturgess laughed. "You know this is not legal?"

"Who gives a shit?" my stepdad said.

"I like the way you do business." Sturgess indicated the builders who were standing around in various stages of excitement, gaping at the turn of events. "What about the witnesses?"

Karl turned to Tony. "I have a hell of a lot of business associates who need construction work done and are willing to pay through the nose for it."

"You can trust us," Tony said, tapping the side of his own nose.

"So, what's in it for me?"

"I'll sign your bloody contract, no questions asked, if I can walk away with Brady at the end of the day."

"Done." Karl offered his hand.

Sturgess held firm. "One proviso."

"What is it?"

"I want to see you fuck Brady's ass."

"I don't do faggot shit," my stepdad spat.

Sturgess withdrew his hand. "No deal then."

Tony, who had had dollar signs in his eyes minutes earlier, saw his golden future tarnishing by the second. "Look at his hole," he said hypnotically, spreading my aching legs wide. "Just ripe for a hot fuck. Think how it will feel having your big meaty cock ploughing his asshole."

"Deep down," Sturgess whispered, "you always knew your stepson was a slut, waiting for you to dump your seed inside him."

Karl seemed uncertain. He must have been weighing up the pros and cons of the deal, screwing his face up in disgust as a bubble of spunk oozed from my hole. Karl spat bitterly. "Your mom was a whore, too. You look just like her lying there like that."

"What's the only way to treat whores?" Sturgess asked.

"Fuck 'em," Tony answered.

Sturgess held my ass cheeks apart to give Karl easy access. "It's so simple, Frank. Just sink your cock in your stepson's ass, fuck it like you would a cunt. Blow your load and the contract is yours. Not only that, I take the sniveling faggot off your hands and you never see him again."

That sold it. There had to be a lot of cash involved in the deal because my stepdad whipped off his trousers and his boxers, ripped open his shirt, and wearing only his shoes and socks, slam dunked his already-hard cock right into my hole. He was sacrificing me for a business deal. I was merely another disposable part of the transaction. I meant nothing to him. It would have broken my heart except I sealed that part of my life away, burying it so deep now it could never be resurrected.

If I concentrated on my ass, I could get through this. My stepdad's cock was buried in my asshole. I almost blew my load at the thought of it. It was as if every nerve ending was on high depravity alert. "Fuck me," I screamed as I reached up and grabbed Karl's nipples and squeezed. He panted as he worked me over. I was pouring all my expertise into showing him how good I was at giving pleasure. He'd live to regret the day he sold me for thirty pieces of silver. I squeezed my ass muscles every time he entered me until I knew I had him.

"Shit, I never fucked a hole quite like this. So tight." To emphasize the point, he rammed his cock into me harder. "Take it, you fucking faggot cock whore. Take your stepdaddy's cock right down to the root."

The others began whispering a chant to spur Karl on. If it was the only way I would ever get him to love me, I wasn't proud. He roared his contempt by spitting in my face. I loved it and he knew it. And it revolted him that I'd won. He gripped me by the throat and let out a wild yell as I felt his cum squirt inside me. That was enough to push me over the edge. My cock gave a small quiver, and then lashings of spunk shot out of my prick, coating my stepdad's belly. He collapsed on top of me, and I could feel his heart racing. He was totally still for a short time before he got up and extracted his softening cock from my battered asshole. He sat down and stared at me as if I were a piece of slut meat. My ass was still exposed and some of his spooge oozed out of my hole. A look of horror crossed his face. It didn't last long before he turned to the priapic construction workers. "Go for it, men. He's all yours. Boys, let yourselves out when you're finished. I'll see you tomorrow to get on with the job."

Karl placed his arm around Sturgess's shoulders to steer him away from the sexual activity. "Come into the other room and we can go over the contract once I've washed the faggot off my cock."

Sturgess shook his head. "You have no idea what you're about to sign away. So be it. Your loss is my gain." The last thing I heard Karl say as the door closed behind him was "Take the slut with you when you go, Sturgess. I don't need a receipt."

As Tony and his workers descended on my battered but willing body, Sturgess stuck his head through the doorway. "Brady, I'm about to buy your freedom."

"My freedom?"

"I don't want you to do anything you don't want to. You're a very presentable young man and it would be a pleasure to have you as a partner. You could help me in innumerable ways."

"But you'd want to fuck me, right?" I was desperate to feel this man inside me again.

"Only if you wanted me to. But there would be others. I need someone who is, shall we say, amenable to helping me close a deal."

I imagined being the play thing of wealthy businessmen. Maybe I could be more important than Karl someday.

"You lucky bastard," Jack said.

I smiled, humming.

"Oh, and Brady, do you have a passport?"

"Of course. Karl always insisted."

"Good. Once the contract is signed, sealed, and delivered, I'll need you in Paris to help with my business interests." He turned to Tony and his workers. "Enjoy yourselves, boys, but don't bruise him. My partners and I don't like to see damage done to one of our own."

VALENTINE'S WAY

"I'm so pissed off with you," Valentine snarled as he wiped the spunk from his lips and licked it from the back of his hand. "You have no idea how pissed off!"

I smirked which just made him all the more angry. But I knew something he didn't.

"All these and none of them from you?" he snapped, waving his hand around to encompass the living room now garlanded with flowers in all shapes and genera – and it was still early. They'd begun arriving about 7am. Valentine had read each card in expectation of a love note from yours truly, becoming more and more furious as time passed.

"I thought Valentines were supposed to be anonymous?" I said.

Valentine didn't find that funny. Because of his name, he took the day very seriously indeed. He pointed to all the blooms that crowded the kitchen bench and the dining table. "Anyone who's ever fucked me and wants a repeat or who has yet to get their cock inside me. They treat me better than my own boyfriend." Just then the security intercom buzzed and Valentine let in another delivery. He welcomed the young lad, average looking and average body, telling him to place the bouquet anywhere he could find the space. Valentine signed the delivery docket then closed his hand over the young man's crotch.

How do you solve a problem like Valentine?

There are as many answers to that as short-term boyfriends he's had. They never lasted but I have. The only way to solve a problem – if you believe there is a problem to start with – is to let him have his own way.

Valentine is one hot man. With that hotness – in body and looks – comes a totally amoral, spoilt brat. He expects to be worshipped and adored by everyone, including me. And I do adore him. Ours is a genuine love match. I know my adoration is returned. In his own peculiar way. The question you should really be asking is not about Valentine but about me. How do I put up with his outrageously provocative behavior? Easy. I may be the sexual top in our relationship but he is in charge of the dynamics. You see, I love to watch Val servicing other men particularly if it's spiced up with a sliver of humiliation for me. It gets me hard. The more Valentine's behavior humiliates me in public the harder I get and our make-up sessions leave us both exhausted and exhilarated.

All I have to do is sit back and wait for the fireworks.

On this particular Valentine's Day he had been doing aerobics to his favorite DVD, clad only in his ass-hugging undies which flattered his hard as steel butt while clinging to his hose-like prick. It didn't hurt that he was naked from the waist up, revealing his washboard stomach, his perfect pecs, and his beautiful biceps;

and from his balls down showing off his lightly blond-haired legs and their perfect musculature. That was just part of the reason I put up with his petty moods and his selfishness. The other was that I loved him.

So I sighed as he unzipped the delivery boy, sinking to his knees to engulf the semi-hard cock in one gulp. The guy looked at me as if worried I might attack him. Valentine took his mouth off the boy's cock, something he hated doing, unless it was about to be inserted in his insatiable asshole, to say, "Don't worry about him, he doesn't matter."

I watched for a while but if Valentine was expecting to get a rise out of me, either emotionally or physically, he was sucking on the wrong cock. Yeah, the kid had a nice weapon but I knew mine was better. Valentine brought him off in next to no time, swallowing most of the spunk but some of it dribbled around the edges of his mouth and on to his hand as the delivery boy pulled out, his knob super sensitive as Valentine kept up the suction. He zipped him up, patted him patronizingly on the butt, and showed him out.

Valentine would have kept up his sulk all day in an effort to shame me for my lack of Valentine's Day spirit, except we were both due to report for our annual charity work – sponsored by the event management company I owned – in about an hour.

There'd been another two deliveries and undoubtedly another two blow jobs as a tip while I was showering. I took delivery of another three while he took his turn in the bathroom, but no one got to sample my oral technique, expert though it is, and they looked disappointed having probably heard on the delivery grapevine that blow jobs were being handed out at our address.

I had a quick look at the cards before removing them from the flowers which we'd drop off at a nearby hospital. Some of the senders had set out to impress, others, who'd been there and done Valentine had gone the budget route with a sickening beg for another chance at Valentine's ass. Avowed enemies of mine pleaded their case florally and even a few friends petitioned for a rendezvous, entreating Valentine to keep their request secret. I was well used to all this backstabbing by now and treated all friends and acquaintances as vicious schemers, until proven otherwise. It made life less disappointing.

Valentine's anger with me had not abated even after a hot shower and he didn't bother speaking as we descended to the car park. It would be a long day as we were both headed to our annual charity volunteering at *The Daisy Chain*, the famed florist in the heart of the gay Golden Mile, run by the equally famous, Willa Catheter, a huge Samoan drag diva who looked a little like a professional wrestler. Willa was a mountain of flesh, a truck driver in a dress. She had a mouth on her that made wharfies blush and a temper famed for having put quite a number of homophobes in their place or else in hospital if they weren't cowered by her stature.

We both loved her to death because she had helped Valentine with a place to crash and a job when he'd first arrived in the city, broke and alone, having been turfed out of home by his rabid dad, a notorious womanizer and fag hater. We had no hesitation in donating our time to the fundraiser, to the extent I even managed to choke the indignity of having to appear in the city streets clad in only a diaper. If you haven't already guessed, we paraded up and down the streets, dressed as cupid, selling a single red rose for charity, at $20 a bloom. Over the years Willa had allowed us to fine tune our costumes so the nappies no longer looked like we were giant babies who'd just taken a dump.

Although initially, Willa had objected when Valentine cheekily streamlined his so that it was more like a pair of tight-fitting flannel undies, until his takings almost tripled the first year he wore it. My only gripe was that after Valentine had been on the streets for an hour of so he kept wedging the back of the costume in his ass crack, thus revealing his provocative tattoo, the one that proclaimed *No Deposit No Return* and in case anyone was slow on the meaning there was a very sexy tattoo arrow in the guise of a devil's tail wending its way across his butt to his asshole. That, in turn, led some prospective buyers to expect a little more for their money than a single red rose.

With Valentine's black mood I almost expected him to go out naked with a banner on his forehead stating Fuck Me Now! He was prone to petulant behavior when he thought he'd been overlooked or slighted. Willa picked up on the tension between us as soon as we arrived at the shop which was packed floor to ceiling with single red roses in clear plastic tubes shaped roughly like arrows, just waiting for *The Daisy Chain* stickers and the charity info to be pressed on. We spent over half an hour getting our flowers together then changing into our cupid costumes in the back room at the shop, before being let loose on the streets of an unsuspecting city.

No, not actually all that unsuspecting. We had become an annual ritual that attracted tourists who happily snapped away at us with mobile phones and video cameras, gawking commuters who stared out from the safety of buses that were funneled down the busy gay street then into the center of the city, and gay men who came out to perv and proposition. We were five in all, splendid examples of gay life. Good looking, well built, hung pleasingly, with dazzling smiles. Four of us were old hands at it, Valentine easily outstripping us in every department, including sales, because he flirted so outrageously even though he always promised me faithfully it meant nothing. This year I dreaded the worst.

Lionel, a thirty-five year old electrician who was still looking for love and thought this was a perfect opportunity to find that elusive boyfriend although anyone he picked up on this jaunt was likely to be gone by the end of the week. Jason, a nineteen year-old twink whom I suspected of harboring an infatuation for the clueless Lionel whose total lack of perception was the main reason why he could never keep a boyfriend. The newbie was Gavin; a tree trunk of a man, a muscle leather aficionado, well over six feet, with muscles that put even Valentine's in the shade courtesy, rumor had it, of steroids. His butt was the most perfect you were ever likely to see, his biceps were veined marvels, and his chest felt like the shiny marble floor of a well-patronized cathedral. I knew because he'd encouraged all of us to have a feel. Valentine, who I could see was in awe of the giant, took the invitation literally and had his hand down Gavin's diaper before he could stop him.

Valentine had tried unsuccessfully to be paired with Gavin, even though he'd confided that Gavin was "average size, and wearing a cock ring," as we left the shop for our allotted corners. I watched Gavin head south, walking as if he had a poker stuck up his bubble butt. He was so tanned it almost looked as if his skin were on the verge of turning to leather. On the strength of his popularity and his previous years' sales figures Valentine had been assigned the prime spot at Taylor Square where two of the city's major traffic arteries intersected and where a number of gay businesses elbowed one another for prominence.

I had the other side of the street where I could keep a watchful eye on him. Willa wasn't stupid, she knew what Valentine could get up to and didn't want him spending his time on his knees, after all this was for charity, moneys raised, bar the wholesale cost of the items being peddled, went to the GLTBQI homeless which meant most people were happy to buy a rose from us. Sales were brisk and Valentine soon emptied his basket of flowers. I'd noticed the steady flow of men who had got up close and very personal as they made their purchases, Valentine waving to me whenever he had men's hands on his butt or his bulge.

Occasionally, I heard a squeal above the roar of the traffic which meant someone had managed to get their finger in his tight little hole. No matter, there was not much they could do on the street, the alleyway Valentine favored for his open air skirmishes was on my side of the thoroughfare and he wouldn't chance passing me for a liaison no matter how pissed off he was. He caught my attention to signal he was going to pick up more stock and would bring some back for me. I nodded as I was almost out as well. I wasn't in Valentine's league when it came to sales but I was no slouch either.

I was a bit surprised, however, when he returned weighed down with roses, forcing what I thought was an unfair proportion onto me. "They're not doing as well down the other end of the street and asked if we could take some off their hands. You don't mind do you?"

The traffic lights had changed and he was off before I'd even had a chance to answer. My sales were slow but steady, Valentine faring much better than me, by my calculation outselling me two to one, if not higher. It wasn't a competition but I wanted to get back to *The Daisy Chain* before him to prepare for the surprise I had arranged. I hoped it would get him out of his shitty mood as well as make him tremendously guilty although that hope was futile as guilt was not a word that sullied Val's vocabulary or a feeling he ever harbored - guilt is totally alien to him.

I watched him go into the pub on the corner. That was okay, we had an arrangement that we could use their toilet during the day and, as it was humid, we'd been drinking copious amounts of fluids, supplied by Willa, who had also handed out salt tablets to us all, calling them 'happy pills'. In fact, Valentine's disappearance made me realize I was also in need of relief. I weaved between the traffic, not waiting for the lights, heading for the bar. I knew Brad, the barman, who offered to look after my blossoms, as he called them. It seems Val had taken his with him, which struck me as rather strange until, descending the stairs to the men's room on a lower level, I passed a number of men going back upstairs all carrying cellophane-encased roses.

Four men were ahead of me in the line outside the door which was unusual as the toilet was commodious and accommodating. Two men came out, both carrying roses. Before the door closed on me, I noticed another three men waiting their turn for the urinal even though the cubicle doors were open, signaling they were vacant.

"What's going on?" I asked the man ahead of me.

"Oh, mate, there's some fuckin' slut in there sucking cock for charity. Word is, he's hot as spunk and got a technique that would make the angels weep. And because it's Valentine's Day he gives each guy a rose," he said.

"How much is the rose?" I asked.

"Nothing, mate. That's free. A blow job costs forty bucks. For an extra ten he swallows."

I really doubted that Valentine would ever spit out man cum. He may pretend, to get the extra ten dollars, but he would never waste it, all the spunk would somehow find its way into his stomach.

Another guy in the line added, "For an extra twenty he'll drink your piss. I hear his throat is pure magic."

Yes, I could vouch for that.

"God alone knows what else the slut will do."

Wrong. I knew better than anyone what Val would do – as yet there had been no limits that I knew of.

More men joined the line behind me but it was moving so fast I was already inside the door. I could just see Val on his knees on the filthy tiled floor near the urinals, as one of the guys held the back of his head and was obviously filling Val's mouth and throat with hot piss because it was spilling from the corners of his mouth, his face and hair a damp and slimy mess.

Valentine burped as the guy withdrew his cock, handed him a rose then announced, "There's no more roses fellers, so hang in there if that doesn't matter and you just want your balls drained."

I'd moved behind the guy in front so Val wouldn't see me. He's usually pretty verbal when it comes to sex but because his mouth was full there was merely the sound of gagging, slurping, grunting and a few half-hearted attempts at porn talk.

I was next in line. I was so turned on watching Valentine slurp up gallons of spooge I was hard and horny, unnaturally so. When my turn came, I moved in to poke my cock in his mouth. He looked me in the eye, then said loudly. "This is for charity, mate. Either pay up or piss off."

I put my head down and jostled my way out of there to the laughter of the waiting line. I heard Valentine tell his admirers, "That loser is my boyfriend" as I made my way upstairs.

"What's going on down there?" Brad asked as he handed over my swag of roses. "Everyone suddenly seems to be needing a piss."

"There's some slut down there sucking cock for charity," I said miserably.

"I'd better get the boss on to it. The hotel could lose its license." Brad buzzed the day manager, and then he turned to me slowly. "For charity? You don't mean...?"

"Yeah, it's Valentine," I confirmed.

"Your boyfriend? That Valentine?"

"Yeah."

"Holy shit! He's hot. Got a reputation as the best cocksucker in town. I gotta get me a piece of that. Sorry, man, I know you're a mate and all but that's too good to turn down. I'm only human." As soon as the manager appeared, Brad raced to the stairs for a slice of Valentine's oral action.

I returned to my corner but business was slow. I wasn't offering what was available just over the road. Valentine appeared about twenty minutes later, a gaggle of men behind him bemoaning the fact they'd missed out, asking when he'd be back again.

"Same time, next year," he called happily, counting his money as he walked back toward *The Daisy Chain*, not even bothering to acknowledge me.

It took another half hour before I'd disposed of all my stock. I was a bit despondent by the time I reached Willa's shop to be confronted by a front door that was locked, a closed sign hanging in the window. It must have been later than I thought. No matter, I went around to the laneway that was used for deliveries. I knew the back door would be open. I was obviously the last as all the other baskets were propped against the back wall.

It seemed to be locked as well but whoever had thrown the bolt hadn't done a good job of it and with a little shoulder it popped open.

Willa always threw a small thank-you buffet at the end of the day in appreciation of our efforts so I knew they'd all be celebrating with champagne and quality finger food. I could hear the laughter and good cheer as I pushed through the door, and moved along the musty corridor that smelled of dead flowers and fetid water.

I was about to call out something totally stupid like "Don't start the party without me," as I entered. I was thankful I hadn't, because the party *had* started without me. They'd obviously been drinking; there were two empty bottles of champagne upturned in ice buckets. More tellingly, Val was face down across the shop counter, one leg on the floor and one raised onto the counter top so his asshole was on open display.

"I hope you boys took your happy pills when I gave them to you because this is one hot fucker and you'll want to be at him for hours," Willa said as she fingered Valentine's ass. I was surprised that he was not trying to prevent the intrusion as we had an agreement that I might turn a blind eye to him pleasuring people orally, but his ass was off limits unless I was there to watch. That's why, pissed off as he was with me, he hadn't peddled his butthole in the toilets at the gay pub. He respected the limits. Now he was allowing a huge Samoan to finger fuck his most intimate parts. The other cupids had already dropped their diapers and were casually playing with their pricks.

Gavin was nervous. "What if his boyfriend shows up?"

Willa laughed. "Unlikely. He's got enough flowers for three. He won't be back for ages. Even if he does manage to get rid of them, he'll come back to locked doors. He'll think Val here has gone home. By the time he works it out we'll have had our way with his boyslut as many times as we want. And, let me tell you, you'll want, once you get a taste of his delicious hole. Eh, Valentine?"

This was Val's opportunity to tell them to stop. Instead he grumbled. "How about a little less talking and a lot more fucking."

Lionel was curious. "Why are we doing this? Todd seems like a nice guy. He's hot."

Thanks Lionel.

"You're welcome to him," Val snarled. "Anyone who forgets Valentine's Day deserves everything he gets. I'm so pissed off that he forgot a day that's so important to me."

Of course, he'd use that as an excuse if he was going to renege on our relationship agreement.

Lionel was still trying to get his head around it. "But how is us all fucking you gonna be punishment for Todd? He won't even know about it."

"Yeah, but I will," Val assured him.

As usual, it was all about Valentine.

"Anyway," he continued. "I'll be full of your spunk. He'll taste it in my mouth; he'll taste it in my ass. He might even taste ass on my cock."

"Won't he know it was us?" Jason asked.

Val laughed. "Not unless he tests for DNA."

"Okay, if you say so," Lionel said. He was eager now. "I want to go first. I've had my eye on your butt for years but I thought you and Todd were happy together. Now I can fuck you guilt free. You're the reason I've never had a proper relationship of my own. No one can live up to you."

Val looked him in the eye, encouragingly. "Now you can fuck me all night if you want to."

"Oh, I want to," he said. He grabbed Val by the neck, pulling him off the counter spinning him around and burying his tongue in Valentine's mouth. Val is a great kisser and Lionel was humming his appreciation of my boyfriend's skills. Jason wasn't about to be left out and saw this as the perfect opportunity to show his mettle. He plunged his fingers into Val's ass, then ascertaining he was anally lubed enough, spread his cheeks before lining his cock up at the inviting hole. He pushed, almost toppling Lionel and Valentine, and was up to his balls before either man knew what was going on.

"Hey," Lionel yelled, attempting to push Jason away, after all he'd reserved first fuck.

There was no dislodging the twink. "Use it or lose it!" he cried out as he pounded away like a young man running for a bus. He'd be done very quickly, but he'd have the stamina to outlast the others on return engagements. Gavin was watching while he toyed with his prick. Yes, it was average, and, yes, he was wearing a cock ring, but it was a very pleasing average and I saw Val lick his lips when he managed to tear his face away from Lionel who was in danger of sucking his mouth off.

"That's it my pretties, give him a good working over, and if mama's happy pills work you should be able to keep it up for days." Willa cackled. "I do like to watch a hot young thing getting a good work out. Plus I wanted to reward my boys for all their hard work today."

"What reward does Todd get out of this?" Gavin asked. "He worked harder than all of us."

"You like Todd do you, Gavin?" Willa raised an eyebrow at his taste.

"I wouldn't say no," Gavin agreed.

"Valentine is way better," she said. "If you ask nicely, and those dick stiffener tablets work their magic, he might even fuck that plump tanned ass of yours."

Willa squeezed it appreciatively then poured more champagne, refilling everyone's glasses then her own. Val gulped his down in one swallow, settling into the raunchy mood in the shop. Willa lowered the lighting so it was more seductive, and moved bouquets and stands to give everyone more room, then sat herself regally in the armchair she reserved for special visitors.

Jason yelled a string of expletives which I took to mean he was blowing a load up Valentine's chute. He withdrew his cock and took the glass of bubbly Willa was holding out to him. "Well done, Jason, my love."

Jason collapsed at her feet, panting. "His ass is amazing."

Lionel wasn't going to miss out on his turn this time and pushed Valentine back onto a bunch of the scattered pillows and quickly hoiked his legs in the air. He positioned his cock head at Valentine's entrance, already slicked with Jason's spooge, and pushed. Lionel gasped as he slid into Valentine's love tunnel. "Ah, fuck, Valentine, it's even better than I thought it would be." His cock was a little on the largish side but nothing Val hadn't accommodated in the past. However, it must have been the rapid entry that made him puff out his breath as if in pain. Lionel leaned in to kiss him while he fucked his elusive prey but, finding it difficult to fuck and kiss, he settled for concentrating on the warmth around his prick.

It's funny how the quiet ones are so noisy when they have sex. Mild-mannered, Clarke Kentish Lionel, who had built up his body to competition level to compensate for his nondescript looks, took to Valentine's hole like an alcoholic to his booze. Lionel was addicted and varied his speed to give both himself and Val more pleasure. As Willa had promised them return bouts, Lionel concentrated on bringing himself off with all speed knowing that the second and third times would be leisurely. Val removed Lionel's hand when he tried to jerk him off simultaneously. He was obviously saving it for a special occasion.

Gavin, whose eyes were glazed with almost the same dreamy passion that Val gets when he's being fucked, moved quickly to lie on the pillows in front of my lover. "Eat my ass, Valentine. Chew my hole. Get your mouth down there and eat me." He lifted his legs to give Val easier access and Lionel, obviously not the jealous type, flipped Val over pushing his face into the tanned butt crevice. He slurped and sucked until he had Gavin writhing on the end of his tongue. I was so hard watching Gavin's sweet butt penetrated orally, his body shivering with passion, his muscles stretching taut and hard, I wanted nothing better than to pounce on top of him and ram my cock right into his man cunt.

Val obviously had the same idea. He arched his body, maneuvering Gavin closer on the pillows so he could line up his cock with that tender inviting asshole. Val doesn't top all that often, maintaining his center of sex is situated in his ass, but he was going to give Gavin a good working over.

Lionel slowed his pace so Val could get in position, waiting until Val had his cock wedged inside the spit slicked hole. Gavin gave no indication of pain of any sort, pushing back to take all of the cock wedged tight in his butthole. It looked awkward at first but eventually they got a rhythm which worked for the three of them. Gavin sighed with satisfaction as Val gave him a right royal buggering, setting the pace, pushing back to impale himself on Lionel then thrusting forward to stick it to the huge tanned bodybuilder.

Lionel pulled Val's head back, biting his neck, yanking his hair roughly while he drilled his hole, then he relaxed allowing Valentine momentum in his mounting of Gavin's muscular butt. Val recognized a submissive when he saw one. He grabbed Gavin's face, squeezing his cheeks until his mouth opened. Val spat a gob of saliva onto the sub's tongue and commanded him to swallow it. "Okay, cunt boy," Val snarled, "This is how it's gonna be. I'm gonna ream your asshole good until you're sorry you ever took cock up that tight butthole of yours. I'll make your pussy muscles so sore you won't wanna be fucked for months. After I blow my load inside you, you'll turn the tables on me, boy, and pound my cunthole in the worst possible way. Got it!"

Gavin grunted his acceptance.

"I didn't hear you, boy!" Valentine bellowed.

Gavin smiled; it gave him a totally evil appearance. "I hear you loud and clear, sir. You are gonna so be my pussyboy till you can't stand it anymore and cry 'enough.' I won't take any notice until I breed your asshole, Valentine. Make you a spooge dump for anybody who wants to unload in your guts."

"Nasty!" Willa relished dirty talk.

"Holy fuckin' shit, you two," Lionel said between gritted teeth. "You sure know how to get a guy to the edge." As if to confirm his diagnosis, he held Val tight around the chest and pumped his groin against his asshole, panting and grunting as if he were spewing his guts inside him. He gave a few final shudders and fell back, his cock plopping out of Valentine's hole, loosening a stream of spunk to ooze down the back of his leg.

That freed Valentine to concentrate on Gavin, nailing him to the floor with his aggressive thrusts.

Jason got up. "I need a piss," he said, scratching his balls. "All that champagne..."

Shit! I was about to be discovered, as the corridor in which I was standing led to the toilet. Unwittingly, Willa saved the day.

"No need to miss this highly entertaining show, Jason, honey. Open up, Valentine, Jason needs a toilet. I'm sure you can oblige.

Don't fuckin' spill a single drop on the floor or you'll be down on your hands and knees licking it clean."

Val loved being used as a latrine so opened his mouth as Jason aimed his limp cock, the stream of hot piss hitting his face before Jason got his aim right. Piss rained down on Gavin's chest and he groaned as he ran his hands through it, putting his fingers in his mouth to suck them dry. Val gulped as best he could, but he wasn't fast enough and it spilled down his chin and over his chest and stomach as he continued to fuck Gavin. Jason wiped his wet cock on Valentine's face. "Cool," he said in admiration.

Gripping Gavin by the throat to make him open his gob, Val spat the residual from his mouth into Gavin's, and then clamped their lips together. The sight was more than cool and I wanted nothing better than to join in but knew better than to attempt it while Val was in one of his moods.

Jason remained where he stood, so when Val and Gavin completed their piss kiss and Val came up for air, Jason shoved his wet prick between Valentine's lips, aiming for the back of his throat. Jason held his head and I could see Val's throat muscles working to milk the hard twink cock. "Jez-us," Jason bleated. "How does he do that?"

Gavin lay still as Jason sank his cock into Valentine's craw.

"Drain my balls. Suck my spunk out, Valentine. Let me see you swirl it around on your tongue and swallow the lot. Here it comes, cocksucker." Jason drew his cock back, squirting thick white gobs of goo into Val's eager mouth. When the last spasm passed, he told Valentine to poke out his tongue so we could see the white juice puddling in his mouth. Val swallowed and it disappeared into his gullet.

Realising it was his turn again, Gavin pulled Valentine against his ass, signalling he wanted the fuck to continue. Val attacked with renewed vigour but I could tell it wasn't happening for him. He seemed to be going through the motions, giving everyone a good time but his heart didn't seem to be in it. He abused Gavin verbally, even slapping his face, then roared as if in triumph as he spewed his load into Gavin's hole. As soon as Val stopped thrusting, Gavin was out from under him, turning him over to top him. Watching these two muscle studs at play was something else. Gavin poked his cock at Val's entrance, sinking all the way in. I could tell from the look on Valentine's face it wasn't getting to the places he wanted it to. For the uninitiated it looked as if it was business as usual but it was a case of the lights being on but no one was home.

When Gavin pulled out after adding another load to those already mellowing in Valentine's chute, Willa parted her legs while she motioned with her index finger that Valentine was to crawl over to her on his hands and knees. She ran her fingers through his hair as he kneeled in front of her. "Not happy, Valentine? What's the matter? You miss Todd?"

Valentine snapped. "He's an asshole, missing the most important day of the year."

Valentine was frustrated. Willa picked up on it.

"It's not much revenge if Todd is not here to see it, is it, Valentine?"

"No, it's not," he said wistfully.

"Still, we won't let that spoil our fun, will we?" she addressed the other men, who all eagerly nodded their agreement.

Willa pulled up her skirt and suddenly there was a hush in the room. She was sporting one of the biggest cocks I'd ever seen.

It was a mammoth pole that jutted straight up from between her legs, previously kept in check by double strength pantyhose and a cock corset.

She had Valentine's undivided attention. She stepped out of her constricting clothes, quickly peeling off her blouse to expose a perfect set of pert female breasts. Willa was all woman from the waist up and all man from the navel down. She sat back down in the chair, now totally naked; stroking her cock like it was a police baton. Val crawled closer until he could have licked Willa's balls.

She ran one of her manicured fingers across the tip of her cock, spreading the oozing pre-come, and then applied it to Val's mouth as if it were lipstick. He licked her finger and she slapped him playfully before applying a second film of cum to his lips so they glistened in the light.

"Tell me, Valentine, what would you say if Todd was here now, watching you on your knees worshipping my cock with your lips shiny with my cum? Just pretend he's here, Valentine. It'll make it so much better for you."

For a moment I thought she knew I was hiding in the hallway.

Val threw his head back and took a deep breath. He stared at a space in front of him, addressing it as if it were me.

"I'm so pissed off with you, Todd. I don't ask much. Just that you remember the things that are important to me. Is it too much to ask? And Valentine's Day is important to me. You know that."

Oh, brother, he was on a whinge binge.

"You don't respect me, Todd. You don't respect everything I do for this relationship. You don't give me space to breathe."

"That's it, baby," Willa encouraged. "Let it all out."

"So, tonight, Todd, I'm having my very own Valentine's Day party with people who respect me, who love me more than you do. My friends."

If Val actually believed any of the shit he'd just sprouted, he was living in a bigger fantasy world than even I had imagined.

Willa pulled Val to her ample breasts to suckle while she played with his ass, obviously zeroing in on his prostate making him grunt with pleasure. Everyone was still hard as a steel rod, especially Willa who had not come yet. She gently, but forcefully, pushed Valentine's head from her breasts toward her cock. He did not object even though there was no way he could get the monster in his mouth without dislocating his jaw. Willa seemed content that he licked it up and down, paying close attention to her balls, engulfing the knob and a few inches of the shaft in his mouth. His oral technique must have been satisfactory because she pulled him off her prick quick smart. "I don't want to come yet, Valentine, although mama's got plenty of loads for you tonight."

Gavin had a look of incredible envy on his face. He wanted Willa's cock and seemed ready to fight for it. Willa told Valentine to jump up on the chair and squat over her prick facing the front so everyone could see it when it sank into his guts. He complied after Willa had greased him from a tube she had on the table beside her. He would need all the lube he could get. He lowered himself slowly until his hole docked with the slimy head of her cock, the veins in the shaft throbbing prominently. I had never seen Val take a cock so large. He tensed as Willa poked it at his puckered entrance, the ring giving as Willa pushed against his sphincter. Valentine screwed his face up in pain. That was a first.

Willa needed to get his attention off the breech to his anal canal. "What would you say if Todd could see what you're doing right this minute?"

He thought about it. "Doesn't Willa have a beautiful cock, Todd? One of the biggest I've ever seen. So hard and juicy. You like to watch your cute Valentine boy getting rammed in the guts by a cock so big it puts your pimple of a dick in the shade?"

That was all it took for Willa to burst her way into his tight cock canal. "Sweet Jesus, your ass is slick, Valentine. I wish you could see my big brown cock busting your hole open. You're such a fuckin' cock pig! I want to ream your hole till you can't stand up."

She might have, too, except for the sudden loud knocking on the front door of the shop.

"Shit! It's Todd," Jason said, obviously concerned considering the way he grabbed for his clothes.

Willa took charge. "Hold on a second. Let's ask Valentine what he wants."

He relished the interruption. "Open the door so he can see me jammed full of cock. Then you guys can hold him down while you blow another load in me."

Lionel looked as if he didn't relish that idea.

"Don't worry," Val assured him. "He's not violent. The most he'll do is storm off in a huff. Okay? So hold my legs up so the first thing he sees is your big brown cock wedged in my ass, Willa. Now, open the door, Gavin."

Willa began to push her monster in and out of Val who began to groan theatrically. "Fuck that feels so good, Willa. It's stretching me so wide I swear you'll split me in two and make my boypussy gape like a spunk dump."

He kept on with the dirty talk as Gavin wrenched open the door, prepared to make a run for it if it became necessary, even though he was stark naked. It was all for naught, for, obviously, it wasn't me at the door.

Standing there was an attractive young lad, in limo driver's livery. I should have been expecting him but in the excitement of the moment I'd forgotten.

"What's going on here?" he asked. He was neither startled nor shocked. Bemused fitted the bill.

"What's it fuckin' look like?" Willa sneered. "Valentine's teaching us all how to knit a cardigan."

In any other circumstance, I may have found that amusing.

Sarcasm didn't seem to faze him. "Is this the slut I'm supposed to pick up?" he asked, nodding in Val's direction.

"Don't tell me," Valentine interrupted. "You're a limo driver and Todd thought all would be forgiven if he hurried home to book you. How pathetic is that?"

"I don't know anything about that, mate." For the first time he got a good look at Val even though he was looking a little the worse for wear by now. "Say, is this a private party or can anyone join in?"

Willa pulled Valentine's legs wider. "Help yourself."

"Don't mind if I do. He's a cute fucker. I'll enjoy slamming him into the ground."

Willa was amused. "If it's all right with you, I'll just finish off inside him and then you can take a turn."

"Fine by me. But I gotta make it quick. I'm on a tight schedule."

She fucked Val so hard she almost knocked him off the chair. I had a perfect view straight between Willa's legs so I could see the strain on Valentine's elastic sphincter that closed tightly round her prick every time she rammed inside him.

"That's one enormous cock," the chauffeur whistled. "And that's one sweet ass taking a beating. Leave a bit of traction for me."

He'd peeled his leather trousers down without taking them off. They hugged his legs so tightly I suspected he needed an hour or more to get into them and wasn't going to jeopardize a ready exit for the sake of comfort.

Once Val laid eyes on the new arrival's prick, it was all over for Willa. The chauffeur's cock couldn't compete in length or thickness or even coloring, but it was a magnificent weapon. Valentine practically drooled. He looked bored with Willa, large as she was, and began to try making her come as quickly as possible. It wouldn't take much more if he was using his muscles to grip every time she entered and pulled out. A few unladylike grunts, a few words I'd never known Willa to mutter before, then Val's ride slowed to a stop. She flopped back as Valentine gingerly dismounted, his asshole leaking badly.

The driver merely pushed him back on Willa's lap, not standing on ceremony, hoisted Valentine's legs in the air, and slid his cock straight in, squelching from the leaking cum bathing his balls.

"How many loads inside him?" The limo driver looked around at the others who were open mouthed at his cheek in coming in and riding roughshod over their polite little gangbang.

"You're number five," Jason said. "In his ass at any rate."

"Yum. Spooge pie," the driver said. "I love sloppy slut holes. Which one of you is his boyfriend?"

Lionel was indignant. "His boyfriend's not here."

"Oh, man. Pity I'm on the job, I could fuck this ass all night."

"Why don't you then? Join us in doing just that," Willa invited.

"Love to but, nah; it's more than my job's worth. Hard to come by such good paying job, especially when you ain't got no skills, like me."

Willa ran her long fingernails across his butt cheeks. "Oh, I wouldn't say you're totally without skills young man."

He looked at his watch; fucked Valentine ultra-powerfully, gave a short grunt, and gritted his teeth for a few seconds, then relaxed. "Probably got time for one more round though. Step up, guys, who's next?"

He pulled Valentine's cheeks apart and cum oozed out of his asshole. Before anyone could stop him, not that they would have, Gavin was on his knees, his lips suctioned to Valentine's well-fucked hole hoovering out the fermenting spunk.

"Nasty boy," the driver said, patting Gavin on the head like a dog. "I like it. I'll know who to come to when my butt needs a good cleaning out."

When Gavin had finished, and while all attention was on the driver, Lionel went for a second attack at Valentine's boy pussy. He was clumsy at lovemaking while buzzing in the utterly forlorn hope of attracting Valentine, instead of just plain fucking him. Valentine got impatient with his ineptitude.

Mr. Limo packed his semi-hard rod away and zipped up before extracting a sheet of paper from the back pocket.

"Yeah, here it is. I'm to pick up a dude named Valentine. Is that you?"

Valentine did his best to nod.

"Cool, Valentine the slut boy. You and your boyfriend, lucky bastard whoever he is. And transport you both, VIP service, only the best for you, Valentine. That's why they sent me, 'cause I'm the best. Transport you with all haste to Club Inferno..." He paused, waiting for the significance to sink in. It did. Everyone stopped what they were doing and turned to the driver.

Jason said what everyone was thinking. "He didn't race home and organize that in an hour or two this afternoon."

Spot on! Club Inferno is the most exclusive gay fuck club in the city, booked out almost a year in advance for Valentine's Day. Admittedly, I pulled a few strings promising the booking manager, a sweet-voiced number named Ethan who squeezed us in after I mentioned Valentine's Z-list celebrity status as the outrageous winning butt boy on the realty web series *World's Best Butt*, a shot at that famed ass. He was panting by the time he'd finished taking my credit card details.

I blanched when he told me the cost but he gave me a discount if I allowed him to bring a friend when he met Val. To my mind the more the merrier.

Val attempted to push Lionel off but Lionel wasn't prepared to give up his prize, probably realizing Valentine was much more interested in the Club Inferno than in him even though his cock was well and truly embedded in the tight hole that continued gripping and teasing albeit on automatic pilot.

Valentine was suspicious. "It could have been organized by someone else, someone keen to get me alone, away from Todd." Turning to the limo driver, he asked, "Does it say who paid for all this?"

The driver consulted the invoice. "Um, says here someone named Todd...um...I can't read the last name."

He showed Valentine the invoice. There would be enough to confirm it was my booking. He slapped Lionel on the butt. "Hurry it up, champ. I don't want to interrupt your pleasure but I've gotta get going shortly."

"When exactly?" Val asked.

"When exactly what?"

"Was it arranged?"

He consulted the invoice again. "First week of January."

Valentine's face lit up for a moment, and then he looked crestfallen. "Oh, shit, he didn't forget. Hell, he'll be so mad."

"Says here, too, I'm supposed to pick up a Special Lovers Bouquet from *The Daisy Chain*. That's here right? You got it ready?"

There was major embarrassment when all eyes turned to Willa.

Valentine voice had just a little too much gravel in it for comfort. "When was the bouquet ordered?"

The driver confirmed what I already knew. "Same time as the Inferno booking."

Valentine turned on Willa. "You knew about this all the time. You knew Todd hadn't forgotten Valentine's Day."

"It must have slipped my mind." Willa smirked, but two of the other three cupids were gathering up their belongings before the shit hit the fan while Lionel was still scaling the peaks to orgasm.

"Okay, you all ready to go?" The driver asked.

"No, Todd's not here. Shit! I've got to find him."

Willa grabbed him by the wrist as he attempted to throw Lionel off. "We got some unfinished business here, Valentine."

"Yeah, and it's gonna stay that way." He was steaming. Willa had not only threatened our relationship, she had almost buggered up something he'd been pestering me about for years.

"I don't think so. I've been planning this for a long, long time, Valentine. Think you can come in here and flaunt your hot ass and I'm just gonna ignore it? Nah, Valentine, you're gonna take my cock over and over again until I say enough is enough." She turned to the limo driver. "Hold him down."

"Not sure if that is part of my duties, ma'am," he said.

"Do what I tell you unless you want to lose all my business."

"Okay, ma'am," he said, hoisting Valentine over his shoulder. "You got that bouquet ready he ordered."

"I'll get it for you after I've fucked the slut's asshole into jelly."

I could see where this was going and took the opportunity to slip out the back door.

About five minutes later I heard the shop open to let out a barrage of expletives that must have turned the air blue, followed by a bottle that shattered on the footpath along with Willa's scheming. She had obviously not got her way.

"And a lovely evening to you too, ma'am," the driver called. I heard Valentine snicker.

"You can put me down now," Valentine said, although he sounded like he didn't mean it. "And you can take your fingers out of my ass." He sounded even less like he meant that.

"Have to keep my fingers in there Valentine boy; I don't want all that spunk dripping over my jacket. Does terrible things to the leather."

"What about the seat in the limo?"

"That's all taken care of, though you maybe have to put on some clothes before you get to Club Inferno."

"I thought Inferno was clothes optional." Val sounded disappointed.

The driver sighed. "Once you're past check-in you can take them off again."

The door of the limo opened and the car shook as Valentine was obviously deposited on the seat. "Up on all fours," the chauffeur muttered.

"You gonna fuck me here?" Valentine laughed.

"Get on your hands and knees, slut," he said, his voice sounded as if it would brook no argument.

There was a period of silence and then I heard a squelching sound. Shit! The driver was fucking Valentine again. I wanted to see this, particularly as Valentine had let out a scream of pain. I, of course, was in the boot of the car. It was not an ordinary boot but a section of the limo behind the seats where the bags were stored. It was necessary because of the number of people who had luggage, fetish gear, or toys they wanted to take to Inferno. I was lying between the back seat and a change of clothes I'd taken the precaution of packing and delivering to the limo company's city office the day before. That had also given me the opportunity to reconfirm the special bouquet with Willa at the same time. Yes, the treacherous bitch knew all about the surprise and had gone out of her way to thwart it.

I had taken the opportunity of lowering one of the arm rests that folded up into the seat and with my finger had managed to make a peep-hole through which I could see the inside of the limo proper. I almost laughed when I discovered the driver was attempting to staunch the oozing sperm by pushing an outsize butt plug into Valentine's asshole which seemed to be resisting at every turn. Eventually, though, he accomplished the task. Valentine didn't seem happy about it.

"There, that should stop you staining the seats."

Valentine was indignant. "I'll bet there's been worse things on these seats than a bit of spunk."

"Yeah, there has," the driver admitted. "And I've always had to pay to clean it up."

"Sorry," Valentine said, sufficiently chastened.

"Have you tried ringing his mobile?"

"It goes to voicemail," Valentine replied.

I'd taken the precaution of turning my cell phone off once I'd retrieved my clothes in the flower shop.

"Did you leave a message?"

"A couple," Valentine admitted. "I'm such a dickhead."

"A very astute observation," the driver said.

"Aren't you supposed to contradict me to make me feel better?"

"Quite frankly, I don't care whether you feel better or not. From the little I know about you, you're a spoilt brat. You think because you've got a great body and good looks the world owes you a living. But the world is full of beautiful men. In fact, most of them will be at Inferno this week. You guys have got it made. You, in particular. You've honed your sexual skills until you're the equal of any courtesan."

"You calling me a whore?" Valentine couldn't keep the pride from his voice.

"Not a common whore, Valentine. Someone who knows everything there is to know about lovemaking. That's what your ass does. It makes love to men's cocks. It's just a pity while you were refining your skills in that direction, you neglected your character."

Ouch. I hoped that wouldn't upset Val too much. I didn't want this occasion spoiled. In fact, it had begun so promisingly when the booking manager had rung me back less than thirty minutes after I'd paid the deposit to Club Inferno over the phone to inform me we'd been upgraded to VIP membership on the strength of Valentine's celebrity. If he discovered that, he'd be uncontrollable.

"Most people love my personalit...uh, what's your name, by the way?"

"See what I mean. You got to know my cock before you knew my name."

"It seemed rather ridiculous to offer to shake hands and introduce myself when you were in such a hurry to bury your cock up me."

The driver laughed. "Yeah, I guess I'm as much to blame. It's Doug."

"What's next, Doug?"

"I'm to take you straight to Inferno."

"What about Todd?" Valentine enquired.

"I thought you'd have more fun on your own."

"That's what everyone thinks but it's not true. He completes me."

"Lots of hot guys at Inferno," Doug said.

"I can have them whether Todd is there or not. He likes to watch. He's proud so many hot guys are envious that he gets to take me home after they've fucked me. I love him watching me. I'm an exhibitionist. It'll be a hundred times better if he's there."

"Ah, I think I understand."

"Sometimes I don't understand it myself."

"Is that why you seemed so bored at the flower shop even though you had that eye-watering pole up your ass?"

"Uh huh."

"But if Todd had been there, forced to watch, that would have made it better. Or if he'd suddenly walked in on you or was spying."

"You do get it," Val said.

"You like to be the center of attention. You like being called a whore and a slut and a cocksucker. Especially by someone Todd knows and doesn't like or who doesn't like him, like that Willa woman?"

"You're in the wrong field of endeavor, Doug."

"We'd better get going; we don't want to miss the fun."

"That's going to be boring with no one to talk to at the club," Val moaned.

"Do me a favor, Valentine. Stop this continual whingeing. There's a whole heap of toys and dirty movies in the back there, courtesy of your boyfriend. Or I can wind the glass screen down so you can talk to me."

"What about any hunky hitchhikers?"

"Strictly against the rules. I could get fired for it. Unless, of course, you demand I pull over and let them in, but you take all responsibility."

"Sounds good," Val said. "I'll leave it in your capable hands, Doug. If you see anyone promising along the way, I command you to stop and allow me to offer them a lift."

"Your command is my wish," Doug said, "but you don't see too many people trying to hitch a ride in the city."

As Doug walked past the back of the vehicle, I heard him speaking on his mobile. "Yeah, boss. Got the slut all tucked up in the van. No sign of the boyfriend. You want me to look? Tried his apartment? Not there? Okay."

It wasn't a long drive but Doug seemed to know every pothole and speed bump on his way. I heard Val try my mobile a few times, each call becoming more and more desperate.

"Please, Todd, ring me. I'm in the limo and we're about to hit the expressway so it will be impossible to turn around and come back for you. Please forgive me. I was stupid. And petty. But it won't happen again, I promise. You can fuck whoever you want at Inferno and I won't say boo. I'll even be celibate for the time we're there. No sex for Valentine and no collecting phone numbers or embarrassing you or disappearing into the cubicles. Just please, ring me. I love you."

I heard a little sob after he hung up from leaving the last message. Then I heard him speak to Doug. "You mind if we stop for a coffee at the next petrol station. They seem to have all sorts of booze back here but no coffee."

"Sure," Doug said. "It'll give me a chance to top up the petrol."

A few minutes later I felt the limo turn off the highway. We ground to a halt and there was a flurry of activity. Valentine had thrown on his T-shirt and jeans. I heard him and Doug in muffled conversation before I was startled by the back of the limo being opened. I tried to wriggle behind the backpacks containing our party clothes.

"How do you take your coffee, mate?" Doug asked.

Before I could stop myself, I replied, "Milk, no sugar. Shit!"

I sat up. It was good to stretch my body.

"It's okay; he's getting something to eat. You can get out and stretch your legs."

I did as he suggested, taking the opportunity of changing into party gear that I had stowed in our bags. I didn't intend going a moment longer dressed as a cherub.

"You must think I'm fucked," I said.

"Nah, you're pissed off at the way he treated you. If it's any consolation I would be, too."

"You knew I was in there all the time?"

"I had a fair idea. The way the limo handled. I can usually judge the drag and there seemed to be too much weight for a near empty boot so I put two and two together and came up with one cute boyfriend."

I laughed. "Is that why you went over every pothole and speed hump?"

"Knew you'd appreciate it."

He'd finished filling the tank.

"You won't tell him, will you?"

"No reason I should, is there?" Doug said. "How will you play it from here? Stay hidden? Reveal yourself and say you fell asleep in the back?"

"This is the last stop before the expressway, right?"

"Yeah."

"So this café is gonna be full of people looking for a lift. If I know Valentine he'll be out here in fifteen minutes with an amateur rugby team giving them a lift as well as blowjobs."

"He's that predictable?"

"Oh, yeah. Not always, but his asshole rules his life and when he gets the itch, nothing, but nothing, will stop him until he scratches it."

"I gotta say, it's one helluva butt. Man, the things he does with it."

"His mouth is just as good."

"You not gonna hit me for fuckin' him."

"If I punched everyone who fucked him I'd need a knuckle transplant or I'd be in jail for the rest of my life."

"You were somewhere in that flower shop watching, weren't you?"

"Live porn show before my very eyes," I confirmed.

"What if I wanted to fuck him again?"

I looked him in the eye. "Don't get hooked. There's a lot of guys have got addicted to Valentine, tried to take him off me. A couple succeeded but in the end it didn't last because they didn't manage to crack the code of what made us work."

"I bet I could," he said.

"Anyone could if they just took the time. That's not to belittle your perception. You're a natural. All it requires is observation to see what makes our relationship tick. But, if you want him on a permanent basis, you gotta put in the hard yards."

"Nah, I can see why some people would want that but not me. Sure, I'd like to spank the selfish little bastard, but I bet there's a few tricks I could teach him to make him appreciate you better."

"He promised me faithfully that if we ever got tickets he'd be celibate at Inferno."

"And will he?" Doug asked.

"Not a snowball's chance in hell."

"But it will get you hard watching him break his promise?"

My breath hitched at the thought. "Oh, yeah."

"He's a lucky man. Not many guys would do what you do."

"It's not easy," I admitted. "Sometimes it…well, it gets a bit much."

Doug smiled conspiratorially. "Maybe you could use some help from time to time."

"You offering?"

"Maybe. Or maybe I know someone who would be ideal." He hesitated just slightly as if wary of what he was about to say. "Are *you* interested?"

I was intrigued. "Depends on what's on offer. I'm open to suggestions."

"The guys at the…"

Before Doug could offer anything else, he whispered, "Val's coming. Hop back in the car. When we get to Club Inferno, I'll let you out at the entrance and keep Valentine busy circling the car park so you can pretend you've been waiting for him with the tickets. Deal?"

"Deal." I slid back in and Doug closed the lid on me. There was muffled conversation before the car slid out on to the highway and picked up speed. I decided to catch up on some sleep so my energy wouldn't flag during the night.

I was awakened by a flood of light when the boot opened. Doug pressed his fingers to my lips. I got the hint. "We're at Club Inferno."

I scrambled out, keeping low so I couldn't be seen as Doug kept Val's attention from the back of the vehicle as I rushed toward the club entrance. The bouncers were of the brick shithouse variety

— Val would love them — and belligerent with it until I waved the tickets and told them I was waiting for my boyfriend.

"Is he as hot as you?" one of them asked.

"Hotter. And if you play your cards right—"

I was interrupted by the shriek of my name just before a bundle of muscle launched itself at me, grabbing me in the tightest hug. "You're here," he babbled. "I missed you"

"Shit, isn't his boyfriend that hot guy from that reality show?" the bouncer asked his mate.

His mate nodded. "I'm hard just thinking about his sweet ass." As if to demonstrate the truth of his breathless statement, he adjusted his crotch, his excitement obvious in his tight jeans.

As Val and I entered the club I learned into the doormen and whispered, "Play your cards right and you could be plugging that ass later tonight." That fantasy would keep them hard for hours.

Inside it was dark without being gloomy, the narrow entryway leading to a three-story atrium packed with naked and semi-naked guests dancing and…well it was a hedonistic gay club so what did I expect? Club Inferno was synonymous with debauchery.

"Oh my god," Valentine exclaimed, "look at the urinals."

If that was an example of the pissoirs, I was fascinated to conjecture what other facilities were available. The length of one side of the third level was a glass trough into which men pissed before their recycled beer and other liquids swirled down a series of transparent pipes to the floor below showering those water sports lovers who danced and fucked under the steady stream.

A voice interrupted my thoughts. "Ah, I see you're admiring our drainage system." I turned to see a stunning young man, muscles straining under his taut tanned skin, the bulge in his shorts promising Nirvana for some lucky guy or multiples thereof.

"I designed it myself," the stranger said proudly. "Very popular with our fetish crowd."

"Very ingenious," I said. "You must be Ethan."

"At your service." He shook my hand which seemed somewhat formal for the occasion.

"This is Valentine."

Val could scarcely raise his eyes from Ethan's bulge.

"It's a real pleasure to meet you in the flesh, Valentine. I'm a great admirer." As if to emphasize how much of an admirer he was, Ethan's cock seemed to lengthen while he shook Val's hand, refusing to let it go. "Let me show you to the VIP bar. You're our guests this evening so please avail yourselves of anything and everything, and I do mean everything," he placed Val's hand on his prominent bulge, "We want this to be an evening you'll never forget."

Guiding us to a concealed black doorway, he pressed the code into the security pad, telling us to memorize the number, and pushed open the entrance when it buzzed. We were escorted to the hidden fourth level that overlooked all the soft and hard-core action below, action that was captured graphically and in close-up on a number of large flat-screen wall monitors strategically placed around the room. There were about forty men availing themselves of the VIP service.

The lounge itself was luxuriously appointed in the manner we've come to associate with London Gentlemen's Clubs of the

Victorian era. There were even butlers carrying silver trays of drinks and finger food orders. Perhaps they were less Victorian era than the furnishings because they were almost naked. Ethan noticed my gaze.

"Health and safety," he said, "Bar staff have to have their cocks covered."

Val sighed. "A real pity."

Ethan smirked. "Of course, we relax the rules a little after midnight." He signaled one of the waiters and whispered his order. It seemed a matter of moments before the waiter reappeared with two lethal-looking blue cocktails. "Our Club Inferno special."

I took a sip. It was delicious although I sensed the sweetness was there to cover ingredients totally detrimental to my health and well being while at the same time being a libido enhancer.

Val obviously enjoyed the drink and downed it in one gulp after an initial test-taste sip. "What's in it?" he asked.

"Ah, if I told you that, I'd have to kill you."

I thought Ethan was only half joking. He snapped his fingers and seconds later Val had another in his hand. He was smart enough to sip it this time.

"What's it called?" I didn't want to seem too curious so I added, "In case I want to order another one later."

"Most of our cocktails have a fetish associated with their name and color. For example, there's the yellow cocktail—"

"For watersports," Val interrupted.

Ethan nodded. "There's a black drink for the leather crowd, there's a silver drink for the slings, pink for oral, red for anal…well, you get the idea. There's a color chart in the drinks menu."

"And this?" I said holding my drink aloft.

"We call it the Totally Fucked. Only the crème de la crème of Club Inferno dare to drink it. It means you're up for anything."

"Good choice," Val responded.

I laughed. "And if you just want an ordinary old-fashioned cocktail? Something that vanilla people might like?"

Ethan didn't smile this time. "Ordinary people don't come to Club Inferno. House rules. If they do get in then they don't stay vanilla for long."

It almost sounded like a threat.

"How about I show you around?" Ethan put his arm around Val's shoulder. That was a hint I was not invited. Ethan snapped his fingers and a cute twink waiter bustled to my side keeping my attention occupied while Ethan led Valentine to his almost certain...sexual satisfaction. He didn't even notice I was not tagging along.

Still, I had my own little sex slave kneeling at my feet unzipping my trousers eager to get a taste of me. I admit it, I was hard. Just fantasizing about what was likely to happen to Valentine on his tour of the premises had my balls roiling. Even more so when I glanced up at the screens and noticed they seemed to be homing in on Valentine. Exquisite torture.

I sat in one of the comfortable burgundy lounge chairs and allowed my minion to lap at my balls and swallow my cock whole. He was an expert and I loved seeing him gag when I thrust too brutally into his throat. Eventually, I shot a load onto his tongue in order to watch him swallow. He was a very obedient waiter although I'm not sure my drinks weren't doctored because the next thing I knew I was awakened by Ethan. I was somewhat less surprised that I was now naked, my cock at full mast either as a result of the drinks containing erection enhancers or the dream I'd had about Val and his night of debauchery.

"I hear you've made a fan of the young waiter who serviced you," Ethan smirked as he sat opposite me. "He's hoping you might make liberal use of his tight little cunt."

I was still a little groggy but admitted, "There's nothing I'd like more."

Ethan raised an eyebrow. "Nothing?"

I smiled. "Well…"

"I'm sure you'll leave here well satisfied."

I had to ask. "Will Valentine?"

Ethan looked me over carefully. "It's an unusual relationship you have."

I nodded. "Not everyone can make it work like we do."

"You're both genuinely in love." It was a statement of fact, not a question. "You can sense it in the way you act together, and also the way you act apart. To use what has become a cliché since that depressing cowboy movie, 'you complete' each other."

I know a monologue when I hear one so I didn't interrupt.

"Valentine is very charming, very personable. And, from what I've seen so far, totally insatiable. It's a winning combination." He turned his attention to me. "You're smart, also charming, built, hung, and full of the essentials that make a man like Valentine happy. You like to see your man content even if it means other men get to taste his delights. In fact, it makes you hard. I can see that by the way your cock is drooling."

"You don't need to butter me up. I know you've already fucked Val. And probably half your mates have as well. I'm just sorry I missed it."

"I'm sure we can edit together some of the security footage for those movie nights with you and your friends."

If he expected me to be shocked he was in for a disappointment. "Speaking of security, Val was quite taken with your Tom of Finland bookend bouncers. Almost as much as they were besotted by him. I'd consider it a favor if you could—"

I didn't have a chance to finish my sentence because Ethan snapped his fingers imperiously and a waiter scooted over. Again with the whispering. The young man hurried away.

We were silent for a few minutes both, I suspect, getting the measure of the other man. Ethan broke first. "My instincts are seldom wrong. I would have said never wrong but that makes me sound egotistical. I have a good feeling about you and I'd like to make you a proposition."

So that was it. "The answer's 'yes.' You're a good-looking guy and I can say without qualification I'd be more than happy to fuck you into the mattress."

Ethan laughed loudly enough that the staff and other guests stopped what they were doing to look at us. "That's definitely on the agenda, but this is something more serious."

"I take fucking very seriously," I joked.

"I'm sure you do." Ethan said. "But it must get wearying keeping track of Valentine, keeping him safe. I thought Doug the limo driver might have mentioned…"

"We were interrupted. But getting back to your point, it does grind me down sometimes. I wish it didn't have to be so time consuming."

"I may have a solution to that stress."

"Has something happened to Valentine?"

He saw my obvious distress. "Good lord, no, nothing like that."

I relaxed a little.

"This is more in the way of a business proposal."

"He's not for sale."

"Just listen for a moment, then I'll let you have your say."

I grumbled but gave in.

"This year we come up with the not totally original idea of a Club Inferno 'mascot.' A front man for our parties and publicity. Someone who is sweet and sexy and —"

"Fuckable"

"I appreciate a man who gets to the point. So, yes, our front man needs to be a bit on the sexually adventurous side."

"A bit?" I smiled. "You want someone who's cocktail of choice is the Totally Fucked."

"That about sums it up."

"It's very olde worlde of you to ask my permission. Although it's appreciated, Val is the person you should ask. I can tell you now his answer will be a resounding 'yes, where do I sign up?' You have no need for concern."

"I've already asked him."

"And he said?"

"To ask you."

"I'll bet he did." I thought for a moment. "What's the sweetener? There has to be one."

"Believe it or not we had every intention of making this offer."

"We?"

"My boyfriend and I own and run this club. We have a relationship similar to yours although not exactly the same. Close enough. We love Club Inferno but it's simply got too big for us. We want a partner to come in and help run the club. We can do the day-to-day stuff. What we need is a front man, and an events manager."

"The club is obviously doing well, so why us?"

"We took the trouble to check up on both of you."

I took a deep breath.

"Before you get all steamed up, hear me out. We had a short list of prospective partners and we had to check out if they were a good fit to our, shall we say, amoral code. You and Valentine romped it in. Miles out in front."

"I'm not sure whether to feel complimented or insulted."

Ethan scribbled something on a paper napkin and slid it across the small table separating us. "Is that an insult?"

I whistled. "Is that for the two of us?"

"Each."

Now I was nonplussed.

"At least you'll know that Valentine is safe. He'll be here or else out doing promotion. You won't have to come up with so many sexual scenarios to keep him amused. They'll occur naturally right here. And, of course, you'll be able to watch any time you like."

"You don't expect me to give up my business?"

"No, this is a part-time position although you are welcome to make use of the amenities whenever you like. Everything, including the staff, is at your disposal."

"As Val will be to the staff."

Ethan nodded. A smile played on my lips.

"What do you think?"

"I..."

A loud fracas downstairs drew our attention to the monitors on the wall. It didn't take much to guess Val would be involved. "What the fuck? That's...oh shit. This is trouble."

Ethan grabbed my arm and hustled me to the elevator. When we got to the second floor all hell had broken loose. I recognized the belligerent guy who was hassling Val.

"What's your problem, Roy? I won, you lost," Val sneered.

"Only cause you wiggled your sexy ass at anyone who you thought could help you win. You're a whore, a fuckin' slut."

Sometimes Val's sarcastic tongue got the better of him. "And you're at Club Inferno because you're a virgin. Right, I get it."

I filled Ethan in on the background. "Roy was the other frontrunner competitor on that realty show Val did. He lost to Val but believes Val let everyone involved with the show tag his ass or cock to win. He's been spoiling for a fight ever since."

"Seems the only guy on the show who didn't get to fuck that pretty ass of yours was me." Roy pouted. "How lucky am I then that I get here and you're drinking a Totally Fucked. Did management tell you that means you're available to anyone who wants? Don't even have to ask permission, just throw you down and fuck you. So, me and my mates are gonna ride your ass until you're so full of our spunk the cum'll squirt out your nose."

"In your dreams," Val said petulantly. Roy was a big fucker and could do a lot of damage. His two mates were likewise.

"Get him boys," Roy ordered and his two goons grabbed Val, pushing him to his knees.

I noticed the two security guys move in but, as yet, hadn't intervened. I looked to Ethan but he seemed oblivious to my concern. This was a tricky situation but I could think of no way of defusing it.

Roy had his cock out and was pushing it in Val's face who was doing his best to avoid taking it in his mouth until Roy whacked him solidly with his larger than normal prick making Val wince. That's what Roy was waiting for and he had his cock in Val's mouth before anyone could blink.

This was a hate fuck. And hot as hell. Roy held the back of Val's head and rammed his cock in and out until Val choked, mucous running out his nose and from the corners of his mouth when he was allowed to breathe. His eyes watered from the pummeling he was receiving.

"You like the taste of my meat, slut?" Roy slapped his face with his slimy cock until Val nodded. "Then you're gonna love it even more up your ass."

Val looked over to me in the crowd and mouthed "Help me." Ethan held me back. But Roy had seen it.

"Who the fuck you asking for help? I don't see anyone coming to help you." Roy was staring down the crowd that had gathered.

"My boyfriend," Val wheezed and pointed directly at me.

"Almost too good to be fuckin' true." Roy turned his attention to me. "I'm gonna fuck your boyfriend's cunt then my mates are gonna take a turn. What do yer think of that?"

I took a step forward. "Over my dead body."

Ethan snapped his fingers, a signal for one of the security guards to grab me. His grip was solid muscle and there was no escape. I was suffocating and could scarcely get a breath. My struggles were more for show than real and the bouncer looked down at me questioningly. I winked. He loosened his grip sufficient that I could rant and rave to my heart's content without having to actually intervene.

Val was already naked so it was easy enough for Roy to push him down on his back on one of the bar tables. Val struggled to get away and it seemed genuine enough but I'd seen him play act the part before.

Val snarled. "Fuck off, you ugly troll. You're never gonna get your cock in my ass."

"Think again, slut." Roy had Val's legs spread, his cock lined up with Val's moist hole, and was in his man cunt so fast that Val let out a banshee wail as if he was being impaled on an elephant. Roy was well hung but I'd seen Val take bigger cocks. Hell, I'd seen him take two at once.

"How do you like seeing your little toy boy fucked by real men," Roy sneered at me.

I struggled valiantly. I cursed, I swore. "I'll make you pay for this. You won't see me coming. My revenge will be brutal and fuckin' painful." I don't think my performance was Oscar worthy but it got the message across.

"Fuck, take it out, it's too big," Val pleaded. He was about as convincing as I was. "Fuck!"

"The sweetest ass I've ever fucked," Roy told his audience, quite a few of whom were already jerking their cocks in appreciation in a different sort of standing ovation. "Hey, guys, don't waste your spunk. Feed it to the slut. Blow it all over his face."

A few onlookers took Roy at his word and managed to dump a load or two in Val's hair and on his face. With one final explosive "Fu-uck" Roy obviously unloaded. He pulled out, a stream of cum following shortly after. One of the party guests was down on his knees suctioning the spunk out before one of Roy's goons could get in position.

Each of them filled Val's ass with cream while I was forced to watch. I was hard as a rock even though a number of partygoers looked at me pityingly.

Val was well fucked after all three had taken a turn but Roy wasn't finished yet. They picked poor fucked Val off the table, his face covered in countless streams of spunk, and dumped him unceremoniously in one of the troughs that showered piss from above.

Roy beckoned to my security guard and I was bundled over to Val who, I thought, looked inordinately pleased with himself while trying to appear broken by the experience he'd just endured.

"What do you think of your boyfriend now?" Roy sneered. "Bet you didn't know he was a cock slut."

Perhaps if I had none of my faculties about me I may not have known but Roy was delusional.

"So show us how you feel about him now."

Don't know what Roy expected but I signaled for the guard to let me loose, then I stepped forward and leaned over to kiss Valentine's slimy mouth. The gasps of surprise from the onlookers were a nice touch. I tongued Val's cum-slimed mouth before whispering, "You want the job?" He nodded.

Standing up, I took my cock in hand and began jerking madly replaying his defilement in my mind. In no time at all I was squirting a load to join the others on his sweet cock-sucking face.

Turning to Roy and his mates, "Maybe you'd like to help me out here. Wash him down." I aimed my cock at Val's face and strained to piss, my bladder full from all the cocktails. Roy and his groupies joined in thinking it was total humiliation for Val and me. They were so clueless. Instead of his face where Roy aimed his flow, I went for his harder than steel cock and pissed on his shaft and his balls. Without even touching himself, Val blew his load as my piss hit the spot.

Ethan smiled contentedly. My face must have looked like an open query because he nodded.

Raising my voice above the hubbub as people lined up to dump on Val in the trough, "Gentlemen. Gentlemen, a bit of quiet please. I hope you all enjoyed our little performance this evening." Roy looked taken aback by the word 'performance'. "But it was our way of introducing you to a new concept here at your favorite bar. Tonight we are unveiling the new public face of Club Inferno. The Face That Sucked a Thousand Cocks. Perhaps I should add that he is also the new public cock and ass of Club Inferno. You'll be seeing a lot more of Valentine around the club. He'd always ready for anything, so show him what you've got. The sky's the limit."

There was much applause and hooting approval. Ethan nodded that I'd done the right thing. Okay, there were contracts to be negotiated and all the legal shit to go through but I only had to look at Val's face, covered in his favorite batter to know I'd done the right thing.

Neither of us would ever forget this Valentine's Day. Nor would Willa when I demanded a refund with penalties on the Valentine's Day bouquet she'd failed to deliver.

WHAT TIME DOES YOUR BOYFRIEND GET HOME?

1. THE REMOVALISTS CAME C.O.D.
[CUM ON DELIVERY]

The sound of loud voices cursing and the thud of something banging against the walls woke me. For a moment I was disoriented until I realized I'd fallen asleep on the couch in my home office. I struggled to recall what happened when I got in last night. I remember coming upstairs to dump my laptop bag and sitting down to take off my shoes, then… That was it. Lights out. I hadn't even contacted Paris, my gorgeous young boyfriend to let him know I would be back a day early I was in such a state when I left my overseas conference for the airport. He hadn't been home when I arrived and I wanted to surprise him and make up for my neglect of late. Too bad he never ventured into my office otherwise he would have discovered me and we could have spent the night in bed together and instead of a dull pain in my back from my cramped posture sleeping on the couch I would be aching in more pleasurable places.

Jumping up to seek him out now, as well as the new day, was a mistake. My head hurt like buggery – well buggery when you don't do it right – and I tripped over a rug that was puddled at my feet. I must have had enough sense to cover myself before I fell asleep although the rug obviously dropped to the floor when I turned over during the night. I was still bushed from too many long corporate meetings followed by too many celebratory drinks and too much back slapping, then more drinks on the plane coming back because I hate flying.

There had been a reason for the rush home but I couldn't for the life of me…

"Watch the mirror, guys," I heard Paris shout in horror. He can be a bit of a drama queen. Still, the thump of furniture hitting a wall or a door brought it all back to me. Of course, Paris was moving in today. After our 'whirlwind' romance of three years, he'd finally consented to give up his tawdry inner-city bedsit and move into my more spacious home – an upmarket mansion complete with manicured grounds and an outdoor pool, more in keeping with his career as an up-and-coming print and catwalk model. If that makes me sound like a prat, so be it. I work bloody hard for the bells and whistles in my life.

Perhaps not enough to keep Paris happy though. "You work too hard," he'd moaned before I left for my latest overseas trip. "I never get to see you." The anthem of neglected spouses the world over. Not that Paris and I were spouses. Yet. He'd baulked at marrying me because of the disparity in our incomes. He didn't want to be seen as my boy toy, and I certainly didn't want to be seen as his sugar daddy. Besides, there is only nine years difference in our ages. He's twenty-two. A very mature twenty-two. I'm a career focused thirty-one. A driven and worldly thirty-one. Up until Paris I'd had no time for emotional attachment. My love was entirely reserved for my career and my advancement.

That all changed when I met him. It was the most boring party I'd ever been to – something to do with company bonding or getting to know the 'little people' who kept the cogs and wheels turning in the lower depths of our multinational corporation. I'm paraphrasing the rather patronizing description of the event by our bloated and be-toupeed Human Resources manager.

I'd been impressed by Paris's opening gambit. I was fiddling with my fifth Scotch on the rocks wondering what I had to do to escape the tedium when a young man whose assets weren't in the rather unprepossessing clothes he wore but in his smile, his model-handsome face, and in the body which his obviously second-hand suit did little to hide.

He leaned in to whisper, "What's say you and I escape this dirge and go fuck in one of the rooms?"

Without waiting for a response, he wiggled his pert little ass as he walked away. I suspect I was drooling as I followed almost as if he was tugging me along by my dick. He found an empty bathroom and by the time I'd joined him and locked the door, he'd managed to divest himself of his clothes and was bending over the bath, his ass slicked and waiting for me. It wasn't until we'd both come twice and made ourselves respectable after one of the most mind-blowing bouts of sexual excess I'd ever experienced that I learned his name. He'd been hired by management to mingle and add a certain tone to the proceedings. And dance with the women, single or otherwise. It took the stress off the non-dancing husbands and boyfriends. But I was the only one that night who managed to get his phone number. And the promise of further escapades of a similar nature.

That part of the bargain was fulfilled although not always in a bathroom. Paris had a propensity to try just about any room in a house or apartment as well as the great outdoors. He obviously had an exhibitionist streak to his nature, turned on by the thought of doing it in public if there was an opportunity we might be caught. His life was as far removed from my own rather staid existence I was immediately caught up in a whirlwind of obsession eventually leading to a mutual attraction that didn't rely solely on our sexual chemistry. We spent hours talking about ourselves. He was bored by my pursuit of economic success while gladly accepting all the benefits of my hard work while I was irritated by his spontaneity and total lack of concern for the niceties of life, although he spent an inordinate amount of time grooming. Usually hogging the bathroom mirror when I was attempting to get ready for work. Apart from that, we were good for each other, smoothing out the other's rougher edges.

It had taken the last two years of sweet talking but now he'd consented to move in with me. We'd both come to the conclusion that it made sense with my heavy workload and his fiscal anxieties. He could concentrate on his career (or lack thereof) and I'd not need to divide my time between his ratty bedsit and my home. A predicted record heat wave for the summer made the decision more palatable for him as his bedsit was like an oven in hell while my home was air conditioned with the added attraction of a pool. I think it was the pool that swung it because he seemed to spend every waking moment he visited poring over fashion magazines, salivating over clothes he would never be able to afford but would look great modeling, whilst lounging in his brief Speedos soaking up the sun's rays, much to the delight of my middle-aged party animal gay neighbors, Morrie and Seth. Sometimes I wondered if they had as many parties of a weekend as they did merely so they and their friends could ogle the taut, tanned and terrific Paris in his cock and ass-hugging swimmers by the pool.

They seemed particularly put out if Paris wasn't around, so much so that if pouting were an Olympic sport they would have won gold. What must have peeved them even more was their welcome bottle of expensive bubbly didn't pan out when they made their very kind offer of...

Morrie ran his fingers up Paris's muscular arm. "Seth and I are modern gay men. We like to share our...ah... attributes."

I couldn't help a skeptical rise in my eyebrow as I looked at their obvious shortcomings. They weren't exactly fat. They had well developed bodies, great pecs and arms, but a slight bulge around the middle. And they were hairy. Chest, thighs, and facial hair – neatly trimmed but still hair. Definitely bears.

They'd made no effort to introduce themselves to me years ago when I first moved into the mansion apart from a wave or a brief 'Good morning' over the luxuriant green hedge kept trimmed by a rather bewitching twink called Brink (who on earth calls their child Brink?) with abs of concrete and a butt you could balance a plate on. But the moment they saw Paris as a semi-permanent fixture they were over at the front door, dressed to impress, their shorts showing their so-called attributes in very vivid outline. I should have said undressed to impress because apart from the shorts they were naked, showing off their hirsute torsos. Morrie's rock-hard nipples were pierced with a set of silver bars, and from the looks of their shorts, Morrie's nipples weren't the only things that were hard. Obviously they wished to share what they were showing off with Paris. Neither of us had any idea they were calling in and he'd inadvertently matched their cock hugging near nudity because he was wearing his skimpiest Speedos – the ones that gave him the widest all-over tan. I suspected they'd been spying on him luxuriating near the pool before they came a-knocking knowing he wouldn't have time to change.

It was the neighborly thing to do to invite them in, after all you never knew when you might need help from the people around you.

"Do come in," I said although Paris looked about as welcoming as an open-air wedding to a thunderstorm. He hissed his displeasure at me.

Morrie and Seth did the ooh-ahh thing over the mansion as Paris showed them around and I escaped to make nibbles and pour drinks. They weren't the beer type so it was wine or spirits. After they seemed somewhat disheartened by our meager cellar selection they both decided on a Jack Daniels and ice. By the time I got back to the living room Paris was wedged on the lounge between the two bears and he looked a far from happy Goldilocks about it, especially as they took every opportunity to touch, rub, stroke, or otherwise harass him.

I call it harassment and Paris looked incredibly uncomfortable but perhaps we were misconstruing friendliness. They were a gregarious couple who'd been together for fifteen years and, despite their harassment of Paris, were so entertaining – Seth was a born raconteur – they had us laughing out loud for much of the visit. Together they owned a successful IT company that allowed them to work from home much of the time. That did make me nervous about their intentions toward Paris although he looked less and less concerned as time passed and I noticed a suspicious stirring in his nether regions. I had to be mistaken about Paris's excitement at the prospect of being left alone with two predators living next door. After all, he said he thought they were sleazy.

We told them a truncated version of our lives and our meeting in which they showed more interest than I thought was neighborly. When Paris revealed he was an aspiring model, they turned on the charm.

"That would explain the muscles," Seth cooed as he ran his fingers across Paris's biceps.

"You must work out a lot," Morrie added.

"I try, but I'm awfully lazy when I stay here. The nearest gym is miles away down the mountain. I have to make up for it when I'm back in my own place in the city."

I could almost hear their brains working. Morrie's face lit up. "Say, there's no need to stress when the solution is close at hand."

Seth eagerly joined the conversation. "We have a home gym. Full works. And a sauna. You're very welcome to pop over and use us…" He looked over to me unable to mistake the murderous look on my face. "Make use of our facilities any time you like. We're usually home."

"That would be awesome. Sometimes I need to tone up for an unexpected shoot and I don't have time to go all the way to the gym. Thanks so much, guys." Paris seemed genuinely touched while I was sending out mind vibes: *Don't believe this bullshit. They're just trying to get you alone to…*

That's when they made it painfully obvious about their objective.

"Of course, we like to share." Seth made it quite plain what they liked to share while looking straight at Paris who smiled benignly. No one looked at me. As if suddenly realizing, Morrie rectified his partner's faux pas by turning his smile to me. "We like to share with everyone. You're welcome to come over any time." He dug the knife in. "If you ever have the time."

My stomach filled disturbingly with butterflies at the thought of Paris with these two men. If they were this brazen when I was home what would they get up to when I wasn't? Paris tended to stay over for the duration when I was away on business. Sure, I had security and all the necessary insurance but I'd been burgled in a previous residence and I didn't like the feeling of violation that accompanies your property being broken into and trashed.

Perhaps it was time I invested in a security company to check on the property so Paris could stay in his own place. Was I being selfish asking him to housesit for me? I was away a lot. The breath died in my lungs, I was lightheaded with anxiety. But there was something more that I couldn't quite identify.

It's not that I dislike hairy men, or even open marriages, it's just that Paris and I had agreed to monogamy. We didn't need anyone else for a happy relationship. Paris answered for both of us. "That's a most gracious offer, Seth, Morrie. Very flattering from two gorgeous men such as yourselves." They both preened. "But we're rather old-fashioned like that. We're both monogamous by nature."

Morrie couldn't hide his disappointment. "Well, you know where we are if you change your mind. Either of you." Again he was looking directly at Paris as he said it. I might as well have been invisible.

They made their excuses to leave shortly after that and I heard them mumbling as they made their way next door via a gap in our mutual backyard hedge.

"Pity," Seth mumbled.

Morrie sighed. "What a waste."

Disappointment was obviously assuaged somewhat by Paris's propensity, now that he was a semi-regular fixture, to sunbake in his Speedos near the pool which gave our neighbors eye candy galore. Unsurprisingly, next door became party central, guests ogling Paris over the hedge which was in serious jeopardy of being trampled, calling invitations, flirting outrageously. I could live with that because, truth be known, I was pleased to have such a handsome and well-built boyfriend and I wanted to show him off. It pleased me to be envied because I was the man Paris had chosen to spend his life with. Oh, yes, we'd had that discussion. This was for keeps. We loved each other. Genuinely and deeply. I had no insecurities on that score. I trusted him implicitly. We had no secrets from each other. Let me qualify. No deep, life altering secrets.

Deep down, I was a little insecure. Sure, I liked all the ogling and flirting, and I knew Paris and I were a perfect fit, but...

I couldn't quite put my finger on it. "You don't have to worry," Paris said after one bout of flirting had ploughed a deep furrow on my brow. "It's you I love but it does a boy good to feel wanted every now and then."

My frown wasn't the result of jealousy. Not exactly. Okay, a little. But there was some other intangible emotion mixed in with it. Uncertainty. Would he? Wouldn't he? If the right person came along. The idea made my stomach feel like the ground had opened up beneath my feet. At the same time my cock got hard imagining the worst. I was disgusted with my thoughts and my reaction. Paris was my man just as I was his. Neither of us needed anyone else. Still, when he flirted so outrageously…

****

I HEARD A STRING of swearing from downstairs. Sighing, I resigned myself to the fact I'd better lend a hand. With a great deal of support from any piece of upright furniture, wall or door, I managed to change out of my suit and into more casual clothes. In the en suite bathroom off my office, I splashed some water on my face but it did little to help, and brushed my teeth because it tasted like something of the crustacean variety had crawled into my mouth to die.

Once I'd completed my change, sucked in enough air to convince myself I wasn't still hung over although I'd taken a few precautionary painkillers – just in case – I was ready to help Paris move in his meager possessions. There was ample room for his mementos. I needed him to personalize the house so he felt more at home, having no artistic flair of my own to speak of. Everything before Paris arrived was the result of a design consultant who did very little consulting, merely imposing his stark minimalist vision on my habitat. People marveled at 'my' good taste but I found my home cold and impersonal. Paris brought warmth as well as booty.

The living room downstairs was strangely quiet as I nudged my unco-operative body along the landing to the top of the stairs where I had to pause because I felt like I needed another 78 hours of sleep and an instant course in hangover pain management. My body was riddled with booze and jet lag. Perhaps the removalists had done their job and already vanished. I'd left cash to cover the cost plus a generous tip in the buffet drawer downstairs so that Paris didn't have to worry. He knew it was there. I'd also texted him a reminder before I left.

The sound of drawers slamming and much colorful language meant he'd forgotten and had probably deleted my text from his phone. Paris could be a bit dizzy sometimes, his head in the clouds. I was the practical one. I told him to keep a list but he wouldn't listen. He'd just tap the side of his head and say smugly, "It's all in here." Clearly, on this occasion, it wasn't. If I let him suffer a little it might teach him a lesson.

"I know it's here somewhere," he moaned. A few more drawers slammed in the kitchen.

"Listen, buddy, we don't have all day." At least one of the removalists sounded exasperated.

"You have another job to go to?" Paris asked nervously. It was unlikely they'd resort to outright violence but they could probably be very intimidating if my idea of sweaty furniture removalists was valid.

"Nah, mate," the other said, "but it's the weekend. Hank and me got places to be."

"I can't find the cash my boyfriend left."

"Take another look." The tone was mildly threatening.

"Look," Paris said reasonably. "You're both making me nervous standing over me like this. Why don't you make yourselves comfortable out by the pool." I heard the fridge open and close. "Here. Go relax outside. I'm sure I'll find it quicker that way."

The sound of beers being opened and cans clunked meant that the guys were at least partly amenable to the plan.

"What happens if you don't find it?"

Paris sighed. "Then you'll have to wait until my boyfriend gets home."

"What time would that be?"

"He flies back in from overseas late tonight."

"Fuck that!"

"Then go outside and let me look in peace. Cool off."

"No swimmers, mate."

"You're wearing boxers? Briefs? Jockstrap?"

The silence said it all.

"Then swim naked. No one will see you."

Paris was being somewhat cavalier with the truth because Seth and Morrie would certainly be able to see from their upstairs window or between the side fence hedge. A hedge that had been mysteriously trimmed back more severely than ever by wundertrimmer, Brink, once Morrie and Seth learned Paris was moving in permanently.

There was much mumbling but it faded as Paris herded the two men outside.

"Nice," one of the guys said.

"Take your time," the other added. "And bring Gus and me another beer."

I heard Paris grab two more beers and take them outside to what sounded like two rapidly mellowing removal men. He chatted for a while and I had thoughts of putting him out of his misery until the sounds of whooping and splashing drew me back to my office overlooking the back yard. I'd taken the precaution of an anti-glare screen over the window because it faced west and the sun was blinding in the afternoon so the glass appeared dark from the yard or else reflected the rays right into your eyes. I could see out but no one could see in.

I heard the whump of a large body hitting the water, followed by another. The guys were obviously taking advantage of Paris's invitation. They were both big and burly, bellies that denoted much love of beer and greasy food. Pendulous balls and long fat cocks proved their bellies would be no barrier to showing their girlfriends or wives a good time.

Paris, meanwhile, was back inside, in full cussing mode. "Shit! Shit! Shit! Where the fuck did he say he put it? It's gotta be here somewhere." I heard the kitchen being ransacked wondering why he was concentrating all his energy on the kitchen and hadn't moved to the other rooms. I shouldn't have but I smiled at his dilemma. *That'll teach you*, I thought.

I went to the top of the stairs ready to call out to save him further embarrassment. I'd just explain that I'd been asleep upstairs and was awoken by his swearing. He came out of the kitchen, looking around as if to decide which room to try next before hiving off into the living room. I held back. *Getting warmer.* He opened a few drawers still muttering curses. From my vantage point on the landing, I could see him moving about the living room becoming more and more frustrated. *Getting hot.* He put his hand on the hiding place and pulled out the drawer. *Bingo!* I heard his sigh of relief from where I was standing hidden by a giant fern he insisted broke up the depressing blandness of the staircase. He put his hand in to withdraw the cash when one of the removalists barged in.

"So you find our money yet, pretty boy?" I recognized the voice as belonging to Hank.

WTF? Pretty boy?

Hank was dripping wet from the pool and had a towel wrapped around his waist.

Paris left his hand in the drawer. "Did you just call me pretty boy?"

He laughed. "You gotta've heard that before now. A face like an angel and a body like a Greek god."

Paris fidgeted nervously. "Are you coming on to me?"

"Fuck yeah. Me and Gus took a shine to your ass the moment we saw it. When you bent over to pick up one of the boxes we both got boners. See." He whipped the towel from around his waist to show off his rather impressive hard-on.

Paris whistled his appreciation.

"So, you see, pretty boy, if you can't find the cash to pay us, me and Gus may need something on deposit in order to come back later. Though the deposit's likely to be on you. Maybe even in you. So what's it to be, pretty boy?"

Paris's eyes were fixed on the guy's cock. He removed his hand from the drawer. *Good boy.* But it was empty.

"I've looked everywhere but I can't find the cash. Sorry."

WTF?

"Remind me again what time your boyfriend gets back."

"Not until late. He normally rings when he's at the airport heading home. That takes a good hour when he can find a cab."

"Then you better hop to it, hadn't you. No deposit and we'll have to take the furniture back with us."

"You won't tell my boyfriend, will you?"

"As long as you don't tell my wife."

Paris smiled. "Deal." With that he walked over to the guy and dropped to his knees.

Was this the Paris who swore he'd be faithful? Was he just another slut who would drop to his knees for any hard cock waved in his direction? Who cared? Well, I suppose I did but my inquisitional brain was being over-ruled at the moment by my cock. The rather visceral feeling in the pit of my stomach made the choice easier.

I should have put a stop to what Paris was doing which could potentially wreck our relationship, but I was transfixed by his out-of-character behavior. He knew where the money was. He'd had his hand on it for fuck's sake. So he wanted this. He wanted this rough guy's cock in his mouth – so there was nothing I could do to prevent it. All I could do is watch with a hollow where my heart used to be.

And, WTF, the hardest erection I'd had in years. Ever. As I watched my boyfriend wrap his lips around Hank's thick veiny cock, he slowly moved down the shaft until it must have hit his gag reflex because I could see the spasms in his throat, my cock throbbed and I thought I was going to lose it at any moment. Now was the time to intervene if I was to save our relationship. I could have excused his behavior on the grounds he was harassed into it because he couldn't find the cash to pay for the job, but here he was...

Paris backed off Hank's cock, now slick with saliva. "Sorry." He stood up. "I can't do this. It's cheating."

That's my Paris.

"Only if you get caught," Hank spat. "Now get down there and suck it like a good slut."

Hank pushed him down, smacking his face with his cock.

Paris baulked. "I'm not a slut."

"Yeah, right. You suck like a slut. You're hard as fuck. It's about to bust out of your shorts."

Paris was loving every minute of his humiliation.

Fucking slut.

And my cock, harder than granite, showed I was enjoying watching it just as much.

Fucking hypocrite. You can't hide the truth from your cock.

Paris shrugged as if to admit his complicity in what was happening, once again sinking his mouth around Hank's prick, taking it down as far as he could until his nose scratched Hanks' pubes. It was a sight to see as Hank held the back of his head firm and fucked into Paris's mouth and throat until I thought my boyfriend would explode, saliva drooling out of the corners of his mouth.

Hank released him, Paris's face a mess of tears and mucous, pulled him to his feet and shoved him over the arm of the lounge. "Pull your cheeks apart, slut." My boyfriend did as he was told, not a peep of complaint. Hank wiped the drool off Paris's face, slathering it on his prick before pushing a little of the mucous up my boyfriend's ass. It wasn't much in the way of lube considering what Hank was packing. A little preliminary fingering and then Hank placed his cock against Paris's hole and shoved in brutally. Paris grunted in obvious pain and Hank stilled to let him get used to the burn.

"Gus? Gus?" Hank yelled.

"What?" came the reply from the terrace outside.

"Get your flabby cock inside. The party's just warming up."

Gus made his entrance, his cock as hard as his mate's. "What party?" He copped an eyeful. "Ah, so that's how it is with pretty boy. Loves cock so much he cheats on his boyfriend."

Paris sputtered indignantly between gritted teeth as Hank began his not-so-gentle thrusts. "I've never cheated before in my life. You bastards are making me do this or you'll take my furniture back."

Hank laughed. "Okay, if that makes you feel better."

"Bastard."

Hank was thrusting with more force, slamming the breath out of a groaning Paris.

"Put something in his mouth, Gus. All that noise the slut's making is turning me off my stroke."

"I've got just the thing. Bring him over here."

Gus lay back on the coffee table, holding his thick hard cock upright. Without missing a stroke, Hank walked Paris over to the waiting man to push his head down on Gus's cock.

"Oh, fuck, what a sweet throat," Gus moaned. "I could get to like this slut a whole lot better."

"Maybe we should pop in for a visit regular like when the boyfriend ain't home," Hank panted.

"Suck it, boy. Get your tongue round the shaft. That's it. You sure know how to suck cock, mate."

"You wanna try his ass for a minute?" That was considerate of Hank to share.

"Have you blown a load?"

"Nah. Close but."

Gus was adamant. "You know I don't go for sloppy seconds."

"This ass is so hot and tight I'd go sloppy anything to get inside it."

"Your boyfriend like your ass sloppy with other guys' spunk?" Gus asked. "He whore you out so he can suck our juice right out of your well-fucked butthole."

"It's not like that," Paris complained. "I've never done this before."

The guys laughed.

"I'd say you got a lot of cheating in your future, mate. You're enjoying this too much to go back." As if to prove his point, Gus spat on his cock although it was already well lubricated with Paris's saliva before parting my boyfriend's ass cheeks and sliding straight inside. There was an 'oomph' from Paris but no real complaint before Hank grabbed his hair and thrust his hard cock between Paris's lips.

I didn't know how I felt about the scene taking place downstairs but my cock was in my hand and I was stroking it almost without thinking, just reacting to the animal sex. I was angry that Paris was cheating on our agreement while simultaneously incredibly turned on and also envious that I couldn't be downstairs watching it in close-up so I could see the cocks stretching Paris's hole and the look on his face as he swallowed those thick cocks. But the situation had gone too far to reveal myself now. I dared not move too suddenly unless it drew

BARRY LOWE

attention to my hiding place so I stroked slowly, edging and backing off because, I had to admit, I didn't want this to end.

But no man, no matter how good his technique or his edging, won't cum eventually so with a string of cussing, Gus blew his load in Paris's ass. He slammed harder, holding Paris tightly around the waist in an attempt to bury more cock inside him, eventually slumping over his back as his cock squirts subsided.

"Fuck, mate. You've got the best ass I ever fucked. You could make good money with that." Gus pulled out and slapped Paris's cheek as a dribble of spunk ran down the back of his leg. "He's all yours, Hank."

Hank, whose cock had been dislodged in the throes of Gus's climax, lifted Paris up as if he weighed nothing and laid him on his back on the coffee table, pulling his legs into the air before spreading them. He bent his knees, lining up his cock with Paris's well-fucked hole and slipped in easily with Gus's spunk as lube. "Oh, man, this ass is so hot and sticky just the way I like it." He turned to Gus who was wiping his prick on his T-shirt, getting dressed to leave. "Think we can get his old man to lend this slut to us?"

"You'd like that wouldn't you, pretty boy." It wasn't a question, Gus was stating a fact. "You'd like us to visit you on a regular basis, mate?"

Paris mumbled his reply.

Hank pulled his hair sharply. "What did you say?"

"Yes," Paris replied.

"Louder. Yes what?" Hank was really drilling his ass as he looked him in the eye. Paris tried to look away but Hank squeezed his throat to keep his attention focused. "Yes what?"

127

"I want you guys to fuck me whenever you feel like hot ass," Paris spat. "I want to feel your cocks inside me, making me your cum slut."

That must have been what Hank was waiting to hear because he roared his orgasm so that I thought Morrie and Seth might hear next door. "Fu-u-u-u-ck."

Hank puffed to catch his breath and then slid his cock out of Paris's hole. "Does your boyfriend fuck you when he gets home?"

Paris nodded, sitting up to rub his legs to alleviate the cramp he sometimes gets from being in one position too long.

"Are you a slut, boy?" Hank asked, a sneer on his face, as he dressed not even bothering to wipe his cock. Paris nodded again. "Let's see just how much of a slut you are. You got two loads right up inside your guts. Hold 'em inside you, boy, until your boyfriend gets home. Let him feel our spunk as he ploughs your ass. Think you can do that or are you just a make-believe slut?"

The hesitation before answering meant he was at least thinking it over and maybe even weighing up the repercussions. Finally, he mumbled, "Yeah." Then his voice rose in volume and confidence. "Yeah, I am a slut. I love cock. I loved your cocks in my ass and down my throat. And, yeah, I will keep your spunk inside me until my boyfriend gets home to fuck me."

Gus and Hank had collected their gear and were ready to leave. "Now, kid," Hank said wistfully, "Much as we loved using you like a whore, we got places to go, families to get home to, so if you'd just go to that drawer over there and get the money you owe us…"

Paris snapped. "You bastard. You knew where it was all the time. You used that as an excuse to fuck me."

Hank grabbed him by the jaw. "And when you climb down from your high horse, mate, you'll remember that you knew where it was all along too. You had your hand in the fuckin' drawer so don't give us all this shit. The moral high ground just went through a Force 10 and it's shifted. When you have the guts to admit to yourself you enjoyed...no, you fuckin' loved it, maybe you'll be a happier person. Thanks, mate. Give our love to your boyfriend."

And with that, they were gone.

Paris cursed as he grabbed his swimmers off the floor and headed toward the stairs. "I need a fuckin' shower to get their stink off me." But he had a smile on his face. He stopped as he felt his ass and pushed his fingers inside. I heard him say, "Yeah, I think I enjoy being a slut" as I scuttled down the corridor to barricade myself quietly in my office.

I listened for the shower as I changed back into my travel clothes, grabbed my bag and headed out the front door, closing it quietly behind me.

Two hours later after a pleasant lunch in a café in the small shopping mall less than a mile from our house, armed with a bunch of the reddest roses and a bottle of superb vintage French champagne which would go so well with the chocolate dipped strawberries I had in a colorful boutique carry bag, I arrived home in a cab I'd taken after promising the driver a twenty buck tip when he grizzled about the short distance and the lousy fare. I'd already texted Paris to tell him I was on approach and eager to see him.

He must have heard the taxi pull up as he opened the front door while I paid the driver before he took off. Paris seemed nervous but once I gave him the roses and the rest of the love gifts he visibly relaxed. "I missed you," he said and it sounded sincere. "I wish you didn't have to go away and leave me so often."

"I'm working on it, baby. Just a little longer." I was actually working on it although it would take a few months yet before I could tie up all the loose ends. "Maybe we can take a honeymoon when I get it settled."

Paris's kiss was hungry and I felt my cock harden in my trousers. I hadn't cum while playing voyeur and my balls were aching. I didn't dare rub one out in the toilet at the mall because I wanted to see if he'd keep his promise to Hank that he'd let their spunk ferment in his ass. And as Paris was still in his Speedos I could see he was similarly excited. I hadn't seen or heard him blow his load while he was being fucked either.

Once he pulled me inside the house and we'd fridged the champers and strawberries and placed the roses in water, I picked him up to carry him to the bedroom. Considering how little he was wearing, I had no trouble stripping him naked before he spread out on the bed. I was all fingers as I tore the buttons on my shirt in my eagerness to strip naked to get my cock inside him. It seemed an eternity as he lay there waiting for me. My belly did somersaults in anticipation of what I would find. Was Paris a cheater or a bona fide slut. I wasn't sure which I preferred. No, I had to be honest, there was one answer I really wanted.

Kneeling on the bed, I lifted his ass and parted his legs. When he realized what I was going to do he struggled to escape my grip but I held firm. "I don't feel like that today, I haven't had a shower yet. Let me blow you."

"Nah. Much as I love your sweet cocksucking mouth it's your tight ass I want today." He gave up the struggle without much resistance, looking slightly apprehensive at my reaction to what I'd find inside him. At least I hoped that was the look I read on his face. I parted his cheeks and Paris looked away. Guilt? That gave me the opportunity to do the unexpected, to slide down the bed until I could sink my tongue against his hole. I smelled the funk and tasted the slightly bitter salt of other men's spunk barely held back by his sphincter muscles. I thought I would blow my load there and then my cock was so primed.

Moving back up the bed, I kneeled between my slutty boyfriend's splayed legs, pressing my pre-cum slicked cock against his puckered used hole and pushed. I slipped in so easily and heard the squish of Gus and Hank's spunk as it warmly enveloped my prick.

"You're already lubricated, babe," I said with a smile because Paris had a look of abject terror on his face. I gently moved his head so that he was looking at me. "You missed me, babe. You couldn't wait so you greased up your old standby for when I'm gone. Your vibrator has really opened you up and that lube inside you feels so great around my cock. I don't think I can last."

I felt the huge sigh of relief as he realized he'd gotten away with it. As I plugged his sticky ass, I leaned in to kiss him. Pity he didn't have spunk on his breath, he'd obviously cleaned his teeth. "I love you," I whispered.

2. A MODEL BOYFRIEND

"You know I don't like the man." I was whining. Not one of my finer character traits. I was having my morning coffee before heading off to the office for the day.

"But he's one of the greatest photographers in the business," Paris countered.

"One of the most amoral sleazy bastards around." Paris would have no comeback because I'd just quoted his very own description of Guido Rosselli, fashion photographer extraordinaire.

Paris lowered his head and mumbled, "Yeah, that too."

"So why would you want to work with him? You've told me all those terrible stories about what he's like on a photo shoot?"

"Because if Guido Rosselli uses you then that's as good as a passport to the top of the business. And I need something to boost my career at the moment. It's stagnating."

"Do you have to sleep with him?" It was a legit question given Rosselli's reputation. And Paris's new-found sexual liberation.

Paris was adamant. "No."

"Perhaps I should rephrase that. Do you have to have sex with him?"

The 'No' this time was a little less adamant.

"Do you want to fuck him?" There, my jealousy was front and center now.

"We've pledged fidelity, remember?"

That wasn't much of an answer, especially as I'd inadvertently witnessed just how seriously he took that particular pledge some six or seven months back. He still didn't know I'd seen him. I'd let his non-answer go for the moment. Paris must have realized he hadn't given the sort of reply that would appease me. He added quickly, "This could make my career. It could be the break I've been waiting for. He only uses the best. Plus his campaigns are seen in the most prestigious magazines and on prominent billboards. Designers will take me seriously. Please don't spoil it for me."

"If you really think it will boost your career then I won't stand in your way."

Paris rushed to my side, hugged me and planted kisses all over my cheeks. "Oh, thank you. Thank you."

He was much too effusive. There had to be more to come. He tried the perky approach. "With any luck I may turn up in one of his glamorous art books." Paris watched me closely for my reaction.

Not one to waste his access to the world's top male models, Rosselli usually cajoled them into an extracurricular photo session that included fetish gear, lots of grease and dark make-up, and a sinister ambience in which a group of hot men often threatened a lone blond. It helped Rosselli's reputation, as well as his sales, that there were lots of erections and even the hint of spunk. There was something disturbing about his art photos. That's what the hitch in my stomach was all about.

"Yeah, I've seen those so-called art books." The sarcasm in my voice belied the fact that I frequently used them as fantasy material to jerk off to. I couldn't deny Rosselli was a superb fashion photographer but his art poses were the stuff of genius although his published artistic oeuvre was much too strong for most community libraries or suburban bookshops. And I'd heard there was material he couldn't publish because it was incredibly arousing – to the right audience.

"I'll just tell him I'm not available then."

"His artistic poses are a bit raunchy, you have to admit that."

He hesitated. "I suppose."

"Plus you'll be showing your junk to the whole world including the guys next door once they find out about it."

"That's if Guido even uses me. Besides Morrie and Seth won't know about the book and if they do they probably won't be able to afford a copy. It'll be very expensive."

"Oh, they'll afford it all right." Even if I had to buy them a copy myself.

Something seemed to excite him as there was definite movement in his shorts which he adjusted when he thought my attention was elsewhere. I wasn't sure whether his excitement was over the idea of posing for Rosselli's raunchy photographs, their publication, or the fact the bears next door would see pictures of him in all his naked glory. Perhaps a little of each.

I don't know why I couldn't just admit that the idea turned me on as well. Ever since I'd seen him with the removalists I couldn't help but get excited by the thought of other men taking my boyfriend. As long as I got to watch. Maybe even join in.

Paris scrunched his face up in that little boy look I just can't resist. "You know I wouldn't do anything you wouldn't want me to."

I kissed the end of his nose. "You win."

He pulled away and trotted off happily. "I always do." Then without even hesitating, he added. "The photo shoot is here. Around the pool."

I went after him. "What?"

"I didn't think you'd mind. You said that this house is as much mine as it is yours now. I didn't think I had to ask. Or were you just paying lip service to what you said?"

"I didn't expect you to ask but I would have liked to be informed. Especially as you know my thoughts on Senor Rosselli."

"I thought you might like to watch me in action."

The coffee exploded from my nose choking me enough that Paris patted me vigorously on the back. "What the fuck?"

Paris was laughing fit to burst. "I meant to watch me at work. People think a model's job is easy. It isn't."

"I didn't think you'd want me around because I might make you nervous."

He sidled up to me. "I like you watching me. It turns me on."

"Be a bit of a problem if you're modeling underwear."

"You could always take me aside and help me out."

I had no idea where this conversation was going. "In front of the other models and the photographer, and his assistants?" I raised an eyebrow daring him to go on.

"Well, you have to be a bit of an exhibitionist to work in the profession." He ran his finger down my crotch. I attempted to wrestle his hand away – too late. "Oh, so you do like the idea of fucking me in front of other men?"

I was so flustered I just babbled.

"I'll take that as a yes, shall I? Pity there's no one around at the moment." Paris slowly lowered my zipper, squeezing his hand inside my trousers and my briefs to release my throbbing hard-on. "Maybe I could invite Seth and Morrie over to watch."

I snorted. "They'd do a lot more than watch. They'd want to join in."

"Yeah. They would, wouldn't they?"

I wasn't going to touch that and I didn't have time to think about it too carefully because Paris wrapped his soft lips around my prick and swallowed it all the way down, humming his contentment. Perhaps he was fantasizing Morrie and Seth watching or, better, Morrie and Seth stroking their cocks waiting their turn. My mind wandered, expanding on my fantasy until I peaked, flooding Paris's mouth and throat with my load. It was only then I noticed that he'd been jerking off at the same time and had blown his wad onto the floor.

He patted my satisfied dick and stood, a bit wobbly on his feet. "Wow. That was intense."

"Yeah," I said putting my tackle away and zipping up. "It was."

"Something you were fantasizing about maybe?"

"Watching you in action," I said. "You know, on a fashion shoot or something." Shit, why did I add the 'or something'?

He laughed. "Me too."

I did love him but something changed when I saw him fucking with the removalists. I still couldn't work out what it was. I did know that I didn't want to split up. But what did I want? And why didn't I just tell him I'd been a witness to his betrayal? Could be I was embarrassed to admit I'd been jerking my cock while I watched. Was it that simple? I should I just tell him that I forgive him and that it can never happen again. Or…

"Will you come and watch the photo shoot with Rosselli?"

"I won't be in the way?"

"Who cares? You're giving him the run of your home and pool, I don't think he's got any cause to complain."

I corrected him. "*Our* home."

"It's okay for him to use *our* home then?"

"I thought you'd already told him he could."

He smiled sheepishly. "I may have told him 'yes' tentatively, pending the approval of my boyfriend."

"Tell him your boyfriend approves." I grabbed my coat, my bag, and my car keys, took one last mouthful of coffee, pecked him on the cheek and got out the door. I'd be late if I didn't put my foot down. By the time I got to the office my PA gave me a message to ring home. Paris was all breathless with delight when I answered. He couldn't have wasted any time in contacting Rosselli once I'd given him the green light.

"I've got the date of the shoot. He's had to reschedule around his other jobs cause he's such a busy man. In demand," Paris enthused.

"You don't have to sell his bona fides," I said. "Just give me the date."

The day and time Paris gave me rang a bell. I consulted the diary on my phone. Yep, I had a conference in another city. I wondered if that was why he'd been so determined to tell me how busy Rosselli was. Paris had my schedule right up until the end of the year so he must have known I wouldn't be there. When I said nothing and the pause got painfully long, he confessed. "I know you have a conference that day but can't you postpone or get someone else to go in your place. This is important."

"So's the conference. One of our biggest clients. Another firm is attempting to poach them right out from under us."

"Oh," he said although he sounded less disappointed than I would have expected if he seriously wanted me to watch his fashion shoot.

"I guess I won't get to see you in action after all."

He tried the cheerful approach. "There's always next time." My instinct told me this is exactly the way he wanted it to be, proving it with his next question. "What time will you get home from the conference?" He probably realized that sounded more sinister than a mere enquiry and added hastily, "We might still be at it." That sounded even more suggestive. "I mean the shoot may not be over."

"I'll try to make it back in time. I'll give you a ring from the venue when we're about to wrap up. How's that?"

"Sounds like a plan."

"You going to work on your tan today?"

"Hell, yeah. I gotta look my best for Rosselli." He disconnected the call sounding happier than he expected because I didn't rock the boat.

I'd lied to him. The conference had been cancelled because I'd met up with the company while I'd been overseas recently and had sweet talked them into staying with us, receiving a substantial bonus for my effort. I'd squirreled it away for the holiday I'd planned. Now totally free to watch Paris at work I had a suspicion I would enjoy it more if he didn't know I was watching.

In the two weeks leading up to the fashion shoot Paris was as buzzy as the Duracell Bunny, simply unable to stay still for a moment, wound up so tight I thought his insides would snap. The plus side for me was that he was so horny he would have fucked himself on a fire hydrant if I hadn't been around. Or worse, Morrie and Seth who hadn't relaxed their pursuit of Paris one iota. If anything, they'd increased in persistence although Paris was equally convincing that he believed in monogamy. I was beginning to wonder whether the entire charade was for my benefit and that the worst had already happened. Nah, Morrie and Seth were too convincing as thwarted Lotharios. Frustration oozed out of every pore. I thought they might eventually resort to payment. Or drugs.

But I had other more immediate problems on my mind. Such as, how was I to play the game so I could watch Paris at work unobserved. I had to convince him that I'd left for my conference but double back and sneak into my office. "It's not that I don't trust Rosselli or the other models but better safe than sorry," I explained as I locked the door to my home office and pocketed the key.

He humored me. "Probably a good idea, babe." He was almost bouncing now in his eagerness for Rosselli to arrive.

I was in the middle of a quick coffee and buttered toast when I heard the van pull up. It wasn't my normal breakfast but I couldn't keep anything else down, my stomach was a flock of butterflies. There was a flurry of activity, slamming doors, loud voices, as Paris went to open the front door.

"Senor Rosselli." Paris's voice was so excitedly high pitched I thought he must have ingested helium with his morning coffee.

"Paris, you are looking fabulous as ever." Rosselli knew his way around a compliment. "Is the lucky man your husband still here?"

"He's in the kitchen having breakfast. He'll be leaving shortly."

"Ah, I must thank him for his hospitality in allowing Guido Rosselli to photograph his lovely house and pool."

"Come and I'll introduce you."

"Ah, such a pity he will not have the time to stay and watch a genius at work. And, of course, see his lovely husband at his best."

I heard Paris giggle. "He's not my husband. Yet."

If I didn't know better I would have thought the exchange was scripted.

"He is still a very lucky man to have one of the world's best looking models as his boyfriend."

They came into the kitchen where I'd just finished rinsing my mug in the sink and stacking the plate in the dishwasher.

"Guido Rosselli, this is the love of my life, Arnie Marden." Paris was positively glowing as he made the introduction.

I'm not sure what I expected of Guido Rosselli. He was reclusive for someone as famous as he was and the photo on the back of his art books did not do him justice. He was male model material himself. He was buff, beautiful, and bad news. I could read it in his face. I shuddered as I shook his hand. It wasn't too limp or sweaty, the grip wasn't too tight as if he were in competition to be alpha male. Like Baby Bear's porridge, it was just right. The flicker of his eyes told me he was sizing me up. Call me paranoid but this guy played for keeps. I wouldn't want to be the person who crossed him. I could see now that he was very much the spider to Paris's fly.

"It is such a pleasure, Mr. Marden."

I smiled. "Call me, Arnie. All my friends do."

What a crock.

"Thank you, Arnie. I hope we will become very close in future. I will make your boy one of the most famous faces in the world." As if to emphasize his point he put his hand on Paris's cheek's and squeezed. "Such a pity that beauty is so transient, I must capture it while I can."

Paris blushed. "Your other models are more handsome than I am."

"Handsome, yes. But you are beautiful. There is a difference."

The mutual admiration society was interrupted by what I can only describe as Frankenstein's monster. A tall man with a face so scarred it looked as if it had been stitched together from fragments removed from a jar in the morgue. But there was something compelling about it. He wasn't ugly, nor was he what you'd call handsome. The only word for him was compelling. If his face was a mash up, his body was that of a muscle god. The biceps bulged fit to burst his skin as he carried lighting equipment down the hallway. He was packing muscle everywhere including, by the looks of it, between his legs. I'd read about Bruno, how Guido had paid for reconstructive surgery after a horrendous explosion on the set of an action movie. The film was never completed because the production companion went into liquidation by which stage the partners had siphoned off any cash reserves rather than pay for Bruno's medical bills and rehabilitation.

Guido had used pre-explosion Bruno in his very earliest photographic portfolio and because Bruno had a profile as a top Hollywood stunt man the photographs had been widely circulated. Guido also used Bruno back then on some of his fashion shoots although his colossal body was too large for most of the clothes. As a result it was Guido who stumped up the money when the industry failed. It was also Guido who eased Bruno out of playing monsters on screen when his rehabilitation was complete by offering him a well-paid assistant's job.

Paris called a greeting. "Hi, Bruno, need some help with the gear?"

Bruno smiled. "Nah, I've got this. But thanks for offering." He wandered off toward the back of the house.

Where were my manners? "Would you and the guys like a coffee, tea, soda, water, beer?"

"Not just now, thanks. Maybe later."

"Fridge is stocked. Coffee is on the bench. Just help yourselves whenever you need it. I hope you have a very productive day, Senor Rosselli." Although I'd told him to call me Arnie he hadn't reciprocated with the request I use his first name. Pretentious shit.

"I hope we leave your fine home in good condition, and that you are not inconvenienced too much. What time will you be returning? I ask only because it is a pity that you will not see your lover and the way in which we use him. For the photographs, you understand."

Oh, yes, I understood perfectly.

"I will be late. Very late. I've a long distance to drive. I'll call when I'm leaving."

"That is good. We will make sure we are gone and out of your hair by the time you get home to your beautiful boyfriend. If you are fortunate enough to get away much earlier please let us know and we will wait for you before we complete the photographs."

"That would be fantastic," I attempted to enthuse. "But it's unlikely I'll get to finish before dark."

"A pity." I half expected Rosselli to wipe a fake tear from his eye. His performance was so insincere I couldn't believe he thought I'd buy it.

"Well, babe, I'm off." I swept Paris into my arms and planted a big sloppy kiss on his lips. He wriggled in an attempt to get away, obviously embarrassed in front of Senor Rosselli. It didn't matter, I'd felt his cock, hard as nails, keen to burst out of his jeans.

I made a big production of leaving and as I got into my car, waving one last time to Paris on the front step, a yellow sedan pulled in with what was obviously two male models on board. They saw Paris as soon as they got out of the vehicle and shrieked in recognition before they skimmed their eyes over me and dismissed me almost immediately as someone of little consequence to their careers. "Ricky. Donald. I had no idea I'd be working with you two. Great to see you." And just like that I was forgotten as Paris ushered the two hunks inside. They were both dark to offset Paris's blond. The fashion shoot would be phenomenal. I, however, was more interested in the après-shoot pictures.

I revved the engine, taking off with a squeal of tires although I was going only as far as the shopping mall where I parked inconspicuously behind the large dumper bins. People avoided the area because it stank of fish and grease and other rotting foodstuffs. Then I carried my overnight bag into the toilet at KFC to change into my casual clothes, dumping my suit back in the car. It was a longer jog back to the house as I kept to back streets in case I was seen. The area is quiet during the day as most folk head off to stress city and their well-heeled jobs that will give them a heart attack or an ulcer by their middle age. Just like I was headed that way too.

My timing had to be precise. If I was caught back at the house I had a number of plausible excuses for being there: 'I spilt coffee all over my suit and came back for another' to 'the car broke down and I didn't have my auto club details with me.' That sort of thing. Plausible, but they wouldn't stand up to close scrutiny.

Because Seth and Morrie were away for the morning – Paris had asked specifically because he didn't want them perving over the back hedge – I had access down the side of their property. I heard voices as they set up the lights. I counted, knowing there was Paris, Rosselli, Bruno, Ricky and Donald. They were all there on the terrace so it was safe to slip into the house now and up the stairs unless one of them felt the urgent need to go inside. I was about to do just that when the whispers of the three models drew my attention.

"This is so great we get to work with you," the one I'd identified as Ricky said.

Donald agreed. "Makes it easier when you like the other guys."

"Come on," Paris laughed. "It's not like you have to fuck the other models. You just have to smile and look pretty."

I peered through the gaps in the hedge and saw Ricky and Donald look at each other.

"What?" Paris said impatiently.

"You know about Guido's art shots after the work is done?" Donald asked. I noticed he did air quotes around art.

"Yeah, I've seen the books. Arnie keeps copies in his office upstairs. He jerks off to the pictures. He doesn't know that I know." Paris snickered.

"Yeah, but didn't he have you over to his place to show you what he expects from his models? You know, the famous Not for Publication pictures?" Ricky sounded a little spooked.

"Nah, how bad can they be?" Paris's voice cracked revealing his nervousness.

"And Arnie is okay with what you're doing?"

"He doesn't know."

Ricky put his arm around Paris's shoulders. "Oh, honey, that's why Marty and I split up. Arnie is bound to find out."

"He doesn't mix in the same circles like Marty does. Nah, he won't." Paris didn't sound too sure though.

Donald put his hands up in surrender. "Not our place to give advice. And we sure as hell won't tell."

"Lips sealed." Ricky imitated locking his lips and throwing away the key. "Until I need them later for you know what."

Paris clearly didn't but he was beginning to get the idea. "I thought all that shit was fake."

Before they could continue the conversation Rosselli called them over for instructions.

That was my opportunity. In through the front door and up the stairs so quietly I could hear my heart hammering in my chest. I wasn't sure I was going to enjoy this day as much as I had watching the removalists. Oh well, if anything went seriously awry I could intervene although I didn't like my chances against Bruno. Still, the cops were just a phone call away.

I took up my position at the reflective window but far enough back that no part of my body touched the glass. It was frustrating that I couldn't hear what was going on, after all the soundtrack added to the frisson of…what?… depravity I was about say. But that was all in my mind at the moment.

The bathroom attached to my office had a window that looked out on the back terrace and the pool. I wondered whether I could prise it open a little to hear what was being said. I'd have to wait until the opportune moment when all their attention was focused somewhere else. It was fifteen minutes of set-up later before the perfect distraction occurred to me. I dialed our landline from my cell phone. The phone inside was turned to full volume so Paris could hear it while he lounged beside the pool. The only reason we still had it was because Paris's sister refused to join the 21st century and would only ring landlines.

It rang as loud as a bell, startling the group downstairs. They all looked toward the glass terrace doors as if some creature was lurking. I slowly pushed the bottom of the bathroom window out. It was one of those hinged style windows that pushes out from the base rather than up and down. I could hear them discussing whether to answer the ring but the answering machine picked up and they relaxed.

I went back to my spying and could hear most of what was being said by leaving the en suite bathroom door open. It was only the whispers and asides that escaped my attention.

Boring doesn't even begin to cover watching a fashion photo shoot. I couldn't cope with all the standing around, the costume changes, the make-up, the lights. Paris and his model mates didn't seem to mind and kept up an irritating chirp of mindless chatter to fill in the gaps between set-ups while I marveled at Bruno being able to tune out and focus on the tasks at hand. Rosselli spent most of his spare time yakking on his cell phone parrying calls from clients or seeking updates on the availability of certain models.

I wish I'd remembered to bring snacks. I was starving. And a book — anything — to alleviate the boredom. I suppose I could get out Rosselli's art books and have a good jerk off session over that. So far the action downstairs just wasn't doing it for me. While Ricky and Donald both had superb smooth muscular bodies (Ricky had a smattering of sculpted hair on his chest) and they were definitely eye candy, I simply couldn't stay hard for them.

It looked to me as if the gossip concerning Rosselli's fashion shoots was almost one hundred per cent fantasy. Very self-satisfied and also strangely disappointed (how is that even possible?) that I'd escaped another voyeuristic fuckfest incorporating my man, I fell into a bored sleep on the couch.

Loud voices woke me. Someone was throwing a tantrum.

Rosselli sounded exasperated. "If it won't go down Ricky, go over in the corner and relieve yourself."

"Why should I?" he shouted petulantly. "It was Paris who got me hard, make him fix it."

"Because we need to finish off this last line of clothes and then you can have as much fun as you want."

The arguing went back and forth, getting nowhere fast. I would have suggested a good slap around the head to Ricky but I took a peek and, yes, he did have an obvious problem. His cock was stretching the material in the briefs he was wearing so conspicuously there was no way Rosselli could photograph him like that. They'd reached an impasse when Paris intervened.

"Come on then," he sighed as if this was going to be the most arduous task of his career. He nodded to the corner of the terrace that was shielded a little by creeping vines.

"Nah, get down and your knees and do it here," Ricky demanded.

I could see Paris tense but he must have thought better of arguing. He folded a towel they'd been using as a prop to kneel on and sank down until his face was level with Ricky's prick. This was not something he was doing for love so there was no foreplay involved. He simply pulled down the waistband of Ricky's briefs positioning it under his balls allowing the long thin cock to bob in his face. Paris grabbed hold of the cock to wet it with his tongue before he engulfed it totally in his mouth.

"Fuckin' hell, did you see that? He swallowed it whole. Fuck me." Ricky had quite a mouth on him.

I knew Paris gave good head, I'd been on the receiving end enough times to vouch for his expertise. It wasn't until I heard myself chuckle that I admitted that this is what I'd been waiting for – hoping for. I stripped out of my sweatpants freeing my already diamond hard prick, stroking slowly wanting it to last, wondering why I hadn't swallowed a Viagra or something so I could stay hard and drain my balls all afternoon. Note to self for next time.

Credit where it's due, Ricky knew how to skull fuck. He held Paris still and rammed his cock down my poor powerless boyfriend's throat, the sounds of sloppy gagging abetted by the sight of strings of drool roping like a web from Paris's nose and mouth.

"Here it comes, fucker." Ricky screamed, holding Paris's head tight against his body until he finished blowing his load. Paris gasped for breath, his face covered with drool, his eyes watering. And there was Rosselli taking a close up.

Donald threw Paris a towel to wipe his face. "That's just a taste of what's to come." The rest of the shoot was over quickly and efficiently so Bruno packed away the clothing they'd modeled and set up for extras.

Rosselli ushered Paris to one side. "I did not discuss with you the very special extra photographs I take after the job is completed. I wasn't sure you would be interested. Your boyfriend might object. Donald tells me he has my books. He likes to…" Rosselli imitated masturbation with his fist. "Maybe he would like to see you in my next volume?"

Paris was non-committal. "Maybe."

"You would like to be in my book?"

"Hell, yeah." Paris wasn't playing hard to convince.

"Maybe we not tell your boyfriend."

"That would be good." Paris agreed.

I don't know how the fuck they hoped to keep the book's publication a secret from me.

"You know what my art is all about?" Rosselli prodded.

Paris was honest. "No, I'm afraid I don't."

"No need for fear. It pleases me to defile beauty."

"Yeah?" Paris was uneasy.

As if it were obvious, Rosselli added. "You are the most beautiful here. It is you who will be defiled. And you will be even more beautiful."

I didn't think Paris understood the full import of what he'd just been told but he readily agreed to do whatever Rosselli asked of him.

They were all going to tag Paris but in reality it was all so posed my cock was as limp as a boiled noodle. It looked artistic but it didn't look sexy. At least not from where I was watching and, it seems, not on the ground either as Paris was also moonlighting as fluffer to keep the guys up long enough for the tableaux to be shot. I suppose it didn't help me get excited that both Donald and Ricky were generic pretty boys. They certainly had a quality that the camera picked up on but in the flesh they oozed Barbie.

Until, that is, Rosselli dressed them up as Roman soldiers. Obviously his new art book had an historical theme although I doubt the ancient Romans wore anything as punk or revealing as the costumes that Donald and Ricky changed into. But then, I'm no historian. Even more to the point, Bruno was kitted out as the most lascivious gladiator in history – eat your heart out Russell Crowe. Paris's modesty was covered by little more than a piece of diaphanous gauze that did even less – let's face it, it did nothing – to hide his own substantial bona fides. It, however, drew your eyes straight to his ass.

"Right, Paris. You're inspecting your troops. Only two of them but photoshop will fill in the rest. Your attention is focused on these two soldiers. You've been told they have the biggest cocks in Rome. That's it, feel them. Nice."

Rosselli was clicking away taking shot after shot as Paris really got into the role. I was almost sorry Rosselli wasn't making a movie. "You worship, cock, Paris. It's your whole life. That's it. Great."

Paris was feeling up his fellow models, rubbing his near naked body against them to arouse their libidos while Bruno looked on playing surreptitiously with his own hidden cock. Paris slid down on his knees, licking Ricky's hardening prick, tracing the underside with his tongue until he reached his balls. He repeated the action on Donald until they both stood proudly at attention. They may not have been the biggest, the longest or the thickest I'd ever seen but there was substantial weaponry on display.

Paris looked a little bored by the whole exercise until Rosselli piqued his interest by shouting, "Pick him up, guys, and toss him on those cushions I set up. And be as rough as you want. The rougher the better. You know what I need."

Paris looked momentarily anxious but as Donald and Rick manhandled him into the air before tossing him heavily on the cushions, I saw him smirk. The leather punk costumes they wore gave them a sinister appearance as they smacked their cocks brutally across Paris's lips, finally forcing them into his mouth, holding his head still for a vicious skull fuck.

Hard at last. I'd have to check my motives later for the reason I was turned on by the rough treatment of the man I loved. Maybe I was a bit too into watching beauty defiled. Perhaps, also, because I knew it was all make believe I was into power games. Time would tell. Right now my concentration was on Donald kneeling on all fours as Ricky pushed Paris' face into Donald's ass crack. My boyfriend licked, chewed and tongued Donald's butt hole until Rosselli called it quits.

"Holy shit, Paris, your tongue is as good as a dick. You can rim me all day if you're ever in the neighborhood."

Interesting, Paris never liked rimming ass before. I'd have to introduce that into our sex play, see what happened. Rosselli called for a change of action which saw Ricky lying on his back while Donald poured oil on his fingers – what, they had no Vaseline jelly in ancient Rome? – then pushing into Paris's ass. I almost blew as I saw three fingers disappear inside my boyfriend, praying he'd force a fourth. With extra lubrication, a bit more strength and a grimace or two from Paris, the fourth finger slipped in.

Donald kept up the finger fuck until Paris visibly relaxed. For a moment I thought his fellow models were going to fist fuck my boyfriend, but Rosselli had other ideas. Paris squatted over Ricky before lowering his ass until he felt cock at his entrance. Shifting about, positioning himself at the correct angle, he sank slowly until his tight ass had enveloped the whole engorged cock. The look of surprise on Ricky's face that Paris took it all so easily was priceless. The look on Paris's face was, on the other hand, sheer bliss. He was facing away from Ricky so Donald was able to face fuck him as Paris expertly rode Ricky's cock.

On a signal from Rosselli, Donald pushed Paris backwards, spread-eagled his legs, lining his cock up with Paris's already stretched hole. Paris flinched in anticipation and I recognized his tension. Donald pushed. It seemed a futile effort until, with a scream from Paris and a cry of triumph from Donald, my boyfriend's ass was breached by a second cock.

"Fuck that's tight," Ricky moaned.

Paris seemed out of it as the two guys settled on a rhythm double tagging his butthole. Eventually Paris's pain threshold increased and he was coaxing his co-workers. "Come on fuck me harder. Fuck. Two cocks in my ass is the best feeling ever. Fucked if I'll ever be happy with just one cock in future."

"You're a fuckin' slut, Paris," Ricky cursed. "I never knew you were so hot for cock. I pity your boyfriend."

Probably not the best conversation to throw into a gangbang. Paris stopped, thought about it for a few seconds, shrugged, and screamed, "Who cares? Fuck me like you mean it. Fuck me like I'm a slut whore cock-sucking piece of shit"

They kept it up until Rosselli got all the pictures he needed. "Now, I want you to seed him. Okay, guys, unload inside his ass."

Donald and Ricky must have been edging or else they can cum on demand because with a few grunts and savage thrusts and a bellow from Donald they must have blown their loads within seconds of each other. Paris and Donald slumped exhausted against Ricky.

"Get off ya bastards. You're squashing me."

"Hold it in, Paris. I need you to hold it in," Rosselli instructed.

As Donald's cock slipped out of Paris's ass a small ooze of spunk ran down Ricky's shaft as he also slowly extracted his prick. Paris clenched hard so there was minimum leakage.

"Bruno."

Rosselli's PA stepped up, slid his cock out of the battered leather pouch he was wearing to the gasp of dismay from Paris and awestruck silence from Donald and Ricky. Almost as big as a fist and thick as a soda can, Bruno slicked it up quickly and then hoist Paris's legs in the air before pushing his enormous cock head against my boyfriend's raw ravaged butt and pushed. Paris must have seen stars because his mouth gaped in surprise and not a little pain.

"Fuck he's tight even after the other two fucked him," Bruno grunted.

Paris grasped at the cushions to help absorb some of the thrusts against his ass. He gritted his teeth until the moment Bruno hit the right spot and suddenly his face transformed. That was the moment Rosselli was waiting for. Bruno increased the tempo, Paris grabbing the fucker's asscheeks to urge him on.

"Fuck, best feeling ever. Shit, it's so fuckin' huge. Fuck. Rip my ass open with your monster cock."

It's a pity Rosselli's photos don't come with a soundtrack.

"Come on," Rosselli yelled. "Tell him what you want, what you really want deep down inside."

Paris threw his head back and keened. "Fuck my slut ass. I want cock. All the cock you can give me. Fuck me until I choke on spunk, fill my ass with hot slimy manjuice."

In a frenzy, Paris grabbed Bruno's face, pulling him in for a kiss so passionate it was enough to blister paint. That was all it took. Bruno roared. If his cum was as prodigious as his cry then Paris's guts would have been flooded. Rosselli, obviously quite hard himself now, instructed Bruno to lift Paris without pulling out and carry him across to a special photographic area he'd set up. Bruno placed him down gently, Paris still obviously blissed out from the intense fucking. Donald and Ricky were hard again and tugging at their cocks as Bruno remained stuck tight in Paris's well-fucked hole.

Donald was first to cum, blowing a slime trail across Paris's blissed out face. A few seconds later, Ricky's cum trail landed across Paris's lips and cheeks, striping him. Rosselli was all action, instructing Bruno to pull out quickly. As he withdrew his heavy cock a river of spunk oozed from Paris's gaping asshole. I lost it and shot all over the floor

"Perfect," Rosselli sighed snapping copious shots. As he did so I saw him shudder a few times. He must have unloaded in his shorts just from photographing the debauchery.

I wiped my cock, tucking it back in my trousers before heading for the door, locking it after me and sneaking down the stairs, heading for my car, still dazed from what I'd witnessed.

3. HALLOWEENIES

When Rosselli's book appeared both Paris and I were stunned. The cover of the large format glossy art book was Paris's face in close-up spattered with strings of translucent cum, his mouth parted sensually, his lips glistening as he licked off one of the spunk strands, his eyes distant yet ecstatic, his hair luminous from the fading afternoon light.

The entire book was devoted to Paris's debauchery. Rosselli had titled it after the depraved Roman emperor, Heliogabulus.

Seth and Morrie hurried in from next door clutching a copy of the book like it was pure gold. It was the day of publication so they were very keen. More importantly, I wouldn't need to buy them a copy.

"We couldn't wait. We were first in line at the gay book store. It's the sexiest book we've ever seen," panted Morrie thrusting it and a black marker pen at Paris. They wanted him to sign the inside page to prove they knew the next Male Model of the Year.

Seth ran his fingers across the cover. "It looks so real. How..." Before he could finish the question, Paris replied.

"Glycerine. The same stuff they use in movies to make it look like actors are crying."

Morrie seemed deflated by the news. "What a pity."

"Did you think my boyfriend would slut himself out for fifteen minutes of fame?" I asked.

"The photos inside are so provocative," Morrie said. "Some of those pictures the cock is so close to his hot little ass bud that it's almost as good as actual penetration."

"Almost being the operative word," Paris said without rancor.

"Just think of how many men around the world will be shooting their spunk while looking at your photo."

"Probably licking the front cover of the book."

"Or shooting their fuck juice all over your face." I provoked. "I'm speaking photographically."

"All that spunk."

"What a pity you couldn't collect it. Gallons and gallons of hot man slime and then..."

There was a long pause. I think all four of us had our own fantasy flashing through our mind because when we emerged from our communal daze there were telltale protuberances in our trousers. We avoided one another's eyes as Paris took the book and wrote a dedication, signing with a flourish before handing it back. Seth had watched over his shoulder as he wrote and quickly closed the book when Paris handed it back hoping I wouldn't see. Too late.

To Morrie and Seth, the sexiest neighbors a slutty cover boy could wish to 'have.' Paris xxx.

When the book appeared it was a scandal. As close to hard core porn as it was possible to get without penetration. People discussed whether the spunk was real or glycerine with the majority of commentators coming down on the side of fake jizz. The art reviews were glowing for Rosselli's groundbreaking work which wasn't surprising as there was many a night I would open the book at random and jerk off to the graphic image. I wondered what photographs Rosselli had in his vault – and how I could get my hands on them?

What was surprising was the amount of attention that Paris received. It began with *Who is the gorgeous cover slut on Rosselli's new photo masterpiece?* and it still hadn't ended. Journalists eventually tracked Paris down to out him to the world and the offers rolled in. He was suddenly in demand as a model and an interviewee. The glitterati wanted to know what it was like to be photographed by the Great Rosselli. The prurient public just wanted to know whether any of it was real and what happened on a Rosselli photo shoot. After all, there were all those hard cocks. Something had to give. Or in Paris's case, take.

The ultimate accolade was an influential US talk show host making Rosselli's opus the Book of the Month. There was such a clamor for copies the publisher rushed a paperback edition and a second edition of the hardcover version into the shops. Seth and

Morrie boasted they had a first edition hardcover signed by the model. They'd needed no TV host recommendation. They may have had the book but from their persistence in propositioning Paris they didn't seem to have had the model. I, too, had a number of first editions, still plastic wrapped and pristine secreted in my office. And I still had a happy and contented Paris as a live-in boyfriend though not so plastic wrapped or pristine.

Rosselli, overwhelmed by his sudden mainstream success – till then he had been the darling of the photo erotica set – found his works in demand by collectors and art galleries. As thanks he gave Paris a large signed blow-up of the cover photo which hung in our living room and became the center of conversation with the mounting number of guests we were entertaining. We both knew the fame was fleeting and made the most of it.

Morrie turned to leave. "Oh, before we forget, we're having a Halloween party on the weekend. We'd love you both to come."

Seth whacked him on the arm, punishment for his double entendre. They both giggled.

"A lot of people will be coming. Please say we can add you two to the mix." Morrie looked hopeful.

Paris turned to me expectantly.

Seth went into full sales mode. "We're doing up the back terrace, it'll be so fabulous it'll make you shit rainbows."

Morrie added his tuppence worth. "But it will be a very exclusive crowd. Nothing vulgar."

Paris was enthusiastic. "Sounds like fun. I haven't been to a Halloween party in ages."

As usual it was me that put a dampener on the situation. "I won't be able to make it, I'm afraid. I have to make a long trip to see my sister. She's in some difficulties and needs me to sort it out."

Paris's face fell.

"But," I added. "There's no reason for Paris not to go. He doesn't need to come with me to my sister's. He'd just be bored anyway."

I got a peck on the cheek, Paris scarcely containing his joy.

I noticed Seth nudge Morrie who then asked in the most casual of tones, "How long will you be gone exactly."

"Not sure exactly," I said, amused at their very unsubtle interrogation.

Seth jumped in. "You know just a rough estimate so we don't disturb your sleep when you get back."

"I'd say three days will do it. I'll ring when I'm leaving. It's about a six-hour drive."

Morrie put his arm around Paris's shoulder. "We'll look after your boyfriend while you're away."

That's what I was afraid of. Afraid? Maybe a tingle at the thought they'd fuck Paris. More than a tingle. A full hard on.

"We'll take really good care of him." Seth was so obvious.

I played along. "Don't let him annoy you. He'll be over at your place all the time if you let him. You might have to set a few limits. He doesn't seem to have any of his own."

Morrie raised an eyebrow. "No limits? Interesting."

Paris laughed it off. "He's joking, guys. Of course I have limits." He smiled mischievously. "I just haven't discovered them yet."

"Then we'll just have to help you in that search." So saying Morrie and Seth headed back to their house.

"You really don't mind if I go?" Paris asked when we were alone.

"Of course not, I trust you. It's Morrie and Seth I don't trust."

"Don't worry, I know how to handle them."

I'll bet you do.

Of course, the very first thing I did once I was alone was ring my sister to inform her I couldn't make Halloween with her family. "Something's come up at the office that needs my urgent attention," I lied.

"That's okay," she said, barely suppressed excitement in her voice. "We got some really really good news. Harry's found a new job. He was getting so despondent, you know, what with being unemployed for so long, but he starts work next Wednesday. I know you must have put in a good word for him."

I interrupted before she got too mawkish. "Harry's a good man."

"I know," she said quietly. "And Arnie, thanks for the cash advance. We'll pay you back every penny once we get back on our feet."

"It wasn't a loan, sis. It was a gift."

"We can't accept that sort of money."

"Of course you can, it's what families do. If there's any left put it toward Ellen and Josh's college fund." I heard the tell-tale sniffles from her end of the phone. It was time to go. "Look, I gotta go. You take care. Tell Harry congratulations from me and we'll catch up real soon."

"Bye," she sniveled. She'd be in happy tears mode shortly.

I hung up, satisfied with a job well done. Now to choose a costume because Morrie and Seth's party was a full-on dress-up extravaganza.

Hm, I think something in leather might fit the bill. A helmet of some sort that covers my face.

Paris would not tell me what he was wearing to the Halloween party no matter how many times I begged. "You'll see it when you get back from your sister's because I'll wear it specially for you."

Call me suspicious but I'd bet the costume he'd model for me would not be the one he wore to the actual party. He knew the sort of men who attended Morrie and Seth's soirees. They were hot, hunky, and haveable. I just wondered with his newly discovered appetite just exactly how many he expected to have. I'd even asked Seth for a head count.

"Usually around a dozen although now that we've announced a mystery special guest it might be as high as fifteen to twenty. Nothing lavish."

Nothing lavish? Their parties were so opulent Marie Antoinette would have been asking for advice.

"Don't let Paris drink too much, he gets a bit silly when he's had too many. He gets horny."

"Really?" I could see Seth filing away that tidbit of information to use later. "We'll make sure he drinks just enough. I promise."

I left early the morning of the party. Paris was antsy so it was good to get away. My farewell was perfunctory. I hugged him but he disengaged my arms impatiently. "Won't you be late?" he muttered.

It wasn't worth arguing because he was obviously distracted so I gave him a quick liplock but he pushed me away when I tried to take it to the next level. "Not now. You'll get me all hot and bothered and I've got a million things to do."

My normal reaction would have been to ask 'Like what?' but I had a good idea what those things were, so I went with humor. "Only a million? Must be a slow day."

"What?" Then he realized I was being funny and swatted my arm. "Go on. Go. Leave me in peace. You've got a long drive and I've got to get myself ready."

"You've got almost ten hours until the party."

He glared.

"Okay, okay. I'm going. I'll see you in three days."

He practically pushed me out the door. "Have a safe journey. Give my love to your sister and Harry and the kids."

He waved but was so eager to get back to what was preoccupying his mind he was back in the house with the door closed before I'd even got into my car. My cock was hard as steel imagining what he was up to. I hoped it would go down before I had a fitting for my costume.

Nervous as hell I approached our street hours later, loud dance music blaring from Morrie and Seth's. My home was in darkness so I let myself in, walking upstairs to my office. The light would be seen from next door even with the reflective glass if I turned it on so I was in semi-darkness when I stared down at the guests next door. Roman seemed to be the flavor of the night. The skimpiest togas imaginable. Even then it was a shame to partly cover such magnificent bodies. I couldn't see Paris anywhere but I expected Morrie and Seth would have hidden him away until the party was in full swing.

Unwrapping the package I'd carried home with me, I wondered if I would get away with it. Or would I be totally humiliated. Too late to worry about it now. I stripped off and wrestled the leather straps across my chest and biceps then turned my attention to the sandals with straps that webbed their way up my calves. The leather apron barely covered my prick that was throbbing in anticipation. The golden helmet was light and slotted enough so that it was easy to breathe.

Examining myself in the full-length mirror courtesy of the ambient light from the party next door, I was shocked by the change. I wouldn't have recognized me if I'd run into myself dressed like that. I went downstairs and out via the back terrace door. I would wait for an opportunity to slip through the hedge and ingratiate myself with the other guests without drawing attention to myself.

Fine in theory. I managed the first part of it with aplomb even if I did scratch my ass badly on the hedge as I pushed through. It was the part about not drawing attention to myself that was a failure. I'd managed to grab a drink from one of the trestle tables set up so guests could help themselves. When a loud voice exclaimed, "Fuck me dead. Who is that gorgeous hunk of meat?" I looked around thinking perhaps that Paris had joined the party only to discover everyone was looking at me.

I raised my glass to the hot man who'd paid me such a pleasing compliment and he smiled thinking he was in with a chance later that night. Inside, groups of Romans stood about chatting although there was no sign of my boyfriend or the hosts. I wandered about nonchalantly attempting to look as if I belonged there – well, I did have an invitation – while searching for Paris.

Inevitably, I was upstairs, my excuse if I was caught being that I was searching for the toilet, when I heard the familiar sound of Paris's voice. "Fuck that hurts. Take it out. Take it out."

Considering what I'd seen poked into Paris's butthole in the past with nary a whimper it must be some monster to get him complaining. That I had to see.

Hoping my disguise would hold up and that by shaving my chest, legs and butt it wouldn't occur to them who I really was, I sauntered down the hallway until I reached the door to the room I'd heard the voices come from.

It takes a lot to surprise me these days but surprise me they did. Paris was on his back on the bed and Morrie was extracting a very large black dildo from Paris's ass. He was hissing as the bulbous stem slid free. "Thank fuck that's out. Are you sure this is all really necessary? We could have faked this you know."

Seth was indignant. "This has to be one hundred and ten percent real. People will talk about this party in awe for years to come until it's whispered from generation to generation and becomes as notorious of the emperor you're channeling tonight."

So Paris was Heliogabalus just like Rosselli's book. It was an apt fit.

"Who's that?" Paris said glancing at me in the doorway.

Deflection was my best defense. That, and a voice deeper than my normal speaking tone.

"Say, aren't you that male model everyone's talking about? Named after some fancy city in Europe. Rome. Er, no. London. No."

Paris lost patience. "Paris. It's Paris."

"That's right. I remember now. You're just as fucking hot in the flesh as you are in that arty farty book."

That assuaged him somewhat. He lives for compliments. "You can never get enough praise," he once told me. Living with an insecure male model can be draining. But it has its compensations. Like tonight.

"Can we help you?" Seth said somewhat irritably.

I played the smart ass. "Depends on what you're offering."

Paris snickered and I thought he glanced at my crotch that was thickening as we spoke.

"He meant what are you doing up here?" Morrie responded.

"Just need to take a piss. Looking for the bathroom. Then I heard the sounds of someone in pain coming from this room. Thought I should investigate. Make sure no one was hurt."

"As you can see we're all fine, so—"

I cut him off. "That's a mighty big dildo to have in such a tiny cute little asshole," I said.

"I've had bigger things up my butt," Paris said with pride.

"Wowee," I said admiringly. "And which one of these gents is your boyfriend. I think I read somewhere you had a man." I was digging the knife in.

"His boyfriend can't be here tonight." Seth was barely containing his temper.

"And you two gents are intending to get yourselves a little ass whoopee on the side."

"Just fuck off, will you?" Morrie hissed. "It's none of your business."

Seth tried to calm the situation. "It's part of the surprise we're unveiling downstairs later."

Paris was getting impatient. "Come on, Morrie. For Christ's sake, fuck me. My ass is itching for hard cock. I thought Arnie was never going to leave this morning. So let's get this show on the road."

"What about…?" Seth nodded in my direction.

"Let him watch. Fuck, he can join in if he wants. He sure looks like he's packing."

Morrie ignored me and shoved his dripping cock into my boyfriend's ass. I wondered whether he'd be so cocky if he knew who I was.

"That's it, fuck my slutty ass. Harder, I love your fuckin' cock. Fuck, that feels so good."

Seth stroked as he watched his lover deep inside my boyfriend. "I bet you'd love it if your boyfriend could see you for the filthy cum slut you are."

His boyfriend could see it and, what's more, was loving every minute of it.

"Never thought I'd get my cock in your tight little hole. You're such a fuckin' tease," Morrie panted shoving his cock into Paris as if it was some sort of punishment.

"Wipe the smile off his face if he knew we were breeding your fuckhole, eh?"

I was more turned on than I ever had been before in my life watching our sleazy neighbors talking filth while they fucked Paris. He was loving it. I could hear the little breaths and squeaks he always makes when he's turned on. Morrie was doing him right.

"You're a total cock slut, aren't you boy?"

"I'm your cock slut, Morrie. And yours, too, Seth."

I added breathlessly. "I bet you want everyone at the party to fuck your ass or that pretty face of yours."

"Fuck yeah," Paris yelled. "Bring it on."

"Think you could take all those men? They'd fuck you raw until your ass was ruined." The idea seemed to appeal to Seth.

Morrie let out a string of expletives, rammed his body against Paris's butt and shuddered. After he'd regained control he pulled out carefully, instructing Paris to clench to stop the spunk from escaping.

"Next," Paris exclaimed.

Seth took his place between Paris's legs.

"I've got an idea," Paris said. "You, new guy, come and lie on the bed."

I did as I was told and Paris quickly removed my leather apron so my cock was fully exposed and hard. He kneeled over me and slowly lowered himself onto my cock. The feeling was incredible as Morrie's warm cum squelched around my thrusting prick.

"Come on, Seth. Get your cock inside me. I want you to double tag me with my boyfriend."

I almost choked on my own tongue. "What?"

"Oh, come on, Arnie. You think I wouldn't recognize my own boyfriend, exfoliation or not?" I was speechless. "Great costume by the way. I think you should wear it when we get home. Turns me on. Explanations later. Right now I need your cock in my ass, Seth."

I felt him slide his substantial cock against my prick in Paris's already stretched asshole. With a little grit and determination and a lot of sweat from Paris, Seth finally sank home. I'd never had friction like this before. As Seth pushed in and out he rubbed my shaft as well as stretching Paris's sphincter until I thought it would snap.

"Fuck this is wonderful. I love getting fucked like a tramp. Hell, I am a tramp."

"And I love that you're a tramp, babe." I needed to give him, as well as me, reassurance.

"Amen, to that," Morrie said. "Now get on with it. We have a mystery guest to unveil at the party."

It didn't take long for me to unload in Paris's ass, aided by my boyfriend's filthy tongue and Morrie's lurid responses. Seth squirted his appreciation a few moments later.

"Keep it in, Paris. That's it." He slid the dildo back to keep the spunk soup inside Paris's stretched ass.

I was part of the audience at what became one of the most notorious gay Halloween parties this city ever hosted. Morrie and Seth had constructed a sloping platform about knee high at the lower end and waist high at the other. It was covered with black plastic and a few scatter cushions.

The lights dimmed, Alex North's triumphal music from the movie *Cleopatra* boomed from the speakers around the terrace as four muscle hunks carried what looked like a serving platter upon which Paris was lounging seductively. The guests burst into spontaneous applause and the whisper went round the room that it was Rosselli's model being borne aloft. They placed him gently on the raised platform, Paris's face a facsimile of that blissed out slut that adorned the cover of Rosselli's book.

Morrie removed the dildo from Paris's ass and the spunk he'd kept inside began to bubble from his ass and run down the platform.

"The only thing missing from this tableau is the glistening cum that was on Paris's despoiled slut face in Rosselli's masterwork. It's our great pleasure to invite you, our special audience, to help make Paris a living work of art by showing your appreciation in the only way possible." To illustrate what he meant, he whipped out his cock and after jerking for a few minutes, showered Paris with his spunk. It didn't take long for others to join the melee until Paris had taken every load on his face, his body, in his mouth and even a few in his ass while I watched as proud of my boyfriend as I would ever be. And so horny I wanted to fuck him every which way. But I could wait my turn. I was patient.

4. A STICKY END

Back home the sun's rays hit the blinds we'd kept closed in an effort to get some sleep. I'd refused to let Paris shower so he was covered with dried snail trails of cum, his ass still oozing from the full-on fucking he'd received. Sure I'd licked him and savored the taste of other men who'd made sport with my boyfriend but in the end it was my bed he was in. Our bed.

"How did you know I'd been watching you all this time? And why didn't you say something?" I asked, still puzzled by what had happened.

"Didn't you realize I'd put a rug over you after you fell asleep in your office the night before the removal guys turned up."

"I thought I must have done it before I fell asleep."

"I couldn't wake you. Not even enough to get you to bed. And you smelled of booze. When the guys wanted their money I knew you'd already be awake and probably on your way downstairs because they made such a racket. When you didn't show I thought I'd have a bit of fun by pretending I didn't know where the cash was that you'd left. I just wanted to see what the guys would do knowing full well you'd stop them before anything nasty happened. But then they got horny and, well, they were hot as fuck and I hadn't had a good fuck in weeks and…well, I thought you'd intervene before it went too far. When you didn't stop them and I had a good excuse if you did – they threatened to take the furniture back, that sort of bullshit, but when you didn't stop them I knew you must be turned on by it all. I knew you were awake because I heard you creeping along the landing upstairs. You'd make a terrible burglar."

"What about Rosselli?"

"When Guido wanted to photograph me I thought it was the perfect opportunity for you to watch close up and stop me if it upset you but you chose to watch it from upstairs. Silly bugger. Next time you say you have an appointment you really shouldn't leave your diary lying around with a cross through said appointment, a canceled scrawled above it. And you think I didn't notice you opened the bathroom window?"

I lifted Paris's legs up over my shoulders and fingered his ass still sloppy from the deposits left by the men who'd fucked him. I pushed my cock in slowly feeling his ass clamp down on my shaft. I sighed with pleasure. Is this the sort of relationship I'd always secretly wanted?

"What about the party?"

"I knew you'd never resist an opportunity like that especially when it involved your two favorite people, Morrie and Seth. They really are nice guys under all that sleaze. I told them what I'd been up to and we cooked up the plan. I knew you weren't at your sister's because I rang her to apologize for not getting to see her and the kids for Halloween. She told me you'd canceled because of pressures at work so we only had to wait for a stranger to turn up at the party. And voila."

"I guess I'm pretty obvious, eh?"

"And totally unpredictable."

"You don't mind that I'm a voyeur who likes watching his boyfriend put out for other men."

"Hell, no. That's hot. As long as you don't mind a boyfriend who likes being watched while he fucks other men."

"Hell, no. That's even hotter."

As I plunged my cock even deeper into his sore ass I knew I should contact Rosselli to get a full body print of the fucked and dripping Paris, not just the face on the cover of his book. We'd hang it in the living room — out and proud. That would show the world we were a marriage made in heaven.

ABOUT THE AUTHOR

Naughty or nice? Sugar or Spice? Whatever way you like it, Barry Lowe writes M/M Romance and Erotica that's as addictive and satisfying as your morning cup of coffee. If you like it short and sweet with a happy ending then saucy romance is for you. But if you like a stronger brew with fetish, cuckold relationships, taboo, and all things steamy then try the Erotica – but watch out for the heat!

Go to https://www.facebook.com/barry.lowe.3591

EROTICA BY BARRY LOWE

NOVELS & ANTHOLOGIES

Available in eBook and Print

YOUR BOYFRIEND IS HOT: Gay Cuckold Erotica

BUSTING BILLY'S BUTT: A Gay Erotic Romance

Steve and Billy's monogamous relationship has gone stale until Billy, ever the exhibitionist, shows them a way to spice up their sex life.

THE GRAVY TRAIN: An Erotic Murder Mystery

Someone on the train has an appetite for murder!

A TOUCH OF THE SON: A Gay Novel

Their secret passion will lead them to hell. Will they be able to find their way back?

OMG! NOT ANOTHER GAY EROTICA ANTHOLOGY?

Gay Erotica with a twist

ROUGH & READY: Gay Tough Guy Erotica

BEAR SKIN: Hot Gay Bear Erotica

THE MORE THE MERRIER; Gay Gangbang Erotica

THE BOY IS A BOTTOM: Gay Anal Erotica

BUTT BOYS: Gay Anal Erotica

BAD-ASS BOYS

SELECTED SHORT FICTION
Available as eBooks

STOCKS AND SHARED

CHOCK FULL OF JOCKS

BREEDING MY BOYFRIEND

NEW JOCK IN TOWN

SUMMER AT RAINBOW COVE

I WAS A MALE NYMPHO FOR THE FBI

For all Barry's titles please visit his page at: lydianpress.com

Lydian Press is dedicated to bringing you the finest
GLBTQ erotic literature on the web.

Visit us on the web at:

http://lydianpress.com